I0694209

edition 2

Category: *Experimental / Nature Fiction / Psychodrama*
KvK 34284721 Amsterdam.

***

A west African lion blinked rainwater out of his eyes and raised his head, ear twitching and rotating toward a frequency in the far distance. A lioness slept beside him in the dark, post–coital, eyes firmly shut, her coat soaked against her skin.

His muscular neck strained under a small, matted mane as the sound blended in and out of the static hiss of a torrential downpour on forest leaves. It was the roar of an animal, faint at first, then clearly gaining ground. The distant sound of cracking twigs and branches caused his ears to twitch again. He stood on his front legs, alert and focused, as the lioness opened one eye and raised her head.

The full moon above thick cloud cover barely illuminated the darkness. The landscape was black beyond twenty meters, but the yell became distinct. It was clearly and disturbingly human, close and hostile.

Through a gap in the acacias, a shadowy figure of a man materialized in the darkness, moving violently toward them as the lion stood tall, bared his teeth and hollered a warning roar of his own. The man bellowed at the top of his lungs and charged into him at full speed, showing no hesitation.

***

Flashes of trapezoidal color, bright white yellows and hot pinks mixed with hexagonal blacks, cerulean blue triangles and twisted red shards. The rapidly shifting still images synchronized with a noise resembling steel balls colliding, upwardly increasing in pitch as they lost frictional energy.

A savagely loud binary handshake mixed with sine tones, smashing into a thousand fragments, cascading through a slightly reverberated soundspace, and becoming sawtooths in a concrete tunnel kilometers long. Polygons resembling pieces of glowing stained glass, followed by a strobe of phosphorescent rectangular bricolage.

The noise floor crackled and hummed underneath the abstractions, a cacophonous whirl, a fountain of seizure–inducing white and pink noise, building toward a stream of tall translucent amber shapes on bluish–black, the whining crackle of impossible fireworks exploding in a vacuum.

The sounds and images continued relentlessly in ultra–rapid succession for almost ninety seconds, then suddenly, in a whitewashed blink, fell silent.

"Kmetra!" Echoed over the gallery forest. She looked back, blinking over the trees to see Maisie running down a knoll in the setting sun, away from a brutalist structure with log beams jutting from outer walls. Kmetra turned forward and squinted, dragging a broad, curved scrap of wood with rope tied to two corners. Dozens of meter–width paintings sat on top in a disheveled stack, several of which lay behind, dotting her haphazard path up the river bank.

She zigzagged her way through tiger bush in long, fast paces, the harmattan wind at her back. Her shoes were caked with fresh mud and the lower billows of her indigo robes collected reddish dust. Maisie eventually ascended from the narrow river's valley, gaining ground as Kmetra plowed across the savannah. Breathless, she stopped just ahead of her path, stretching her arms wide and making eye contact.

Kmetra stared through her. A wild painted dog appeared, observing from the grass ten meters to her left. She abruptly turned right, dragging the work over various grass patches as Maisie followed. "You shouldn't be out this far."

Kmetra picked up the pace, her cargo wobbling behind her. "I'm trying to help you," Maisie abruptly stepped on the paintings, halting Kmetra's progress. Kmetra whipped around, the rope taut. "You're going to get me in a lot of trouble!" Maisie pleaded. Kmetra made extended eye contact and said nothing, before aggressively pointing in the direction they had come from.

A hard yank caught Maisie off balance, and Kmetra was off again, losing a painting that crumpled in the grass underfoot. The canine, trotting cautiously behind them, jumped sideways at the sudden movement.

Maisie brushed blonde hair aside, raising a bracelet to eye level with the other arm. She scanned the landscape desperately, her hand over her eyes. Heaving a sigh, she continued with a furrowed brow, reluctantly following the fresh trail in the dirt.

***

Twilight crept in as they reached an elevated clearing. The savannah had transformed into a sparsely vegetated desert landscape. The dog and initial terrain were nowhere in sight. Kmetra paused for a moment, giving Maisie a chance to close the gap between them. A group of children could be heard playing in the far distance, laughter and shouts floating through the arid plateau.

Kmetra dropped the twine tethered to her temporary land-boat. A wide line in the ground shrank into the distance behind it. She began combing through the stack of paintings, a chaotic collection of muted browns, greens, purples, off-whites, burgundy and crimson abstractions, clear color separations between variegated shapes and sizes.

As Maisie looked on, Kmetra walked to a waist high foxtail patch and propped a painting against it. The razor thin textured panel held itself up, and Kmetra continued around the clearing, selecting paintings in seemingly random order and distributing them unevenly across the space, some laying flat, others angled, vertical, or sideways, even buried in a thicket of vegetation.

Two boys appeared, noisily racing and pushing each other in dusty shorts and shirts. They ran across the clearing and into Maisie, one curiously inspecting the dwindling pile of paintings, the other asking a question in Gourmanché. Maisie shrugged her shoulders nervously, the boy's smile a mix of new adult teeth and gaps.

Kmetra remained focused on her jumbled ground collage, roughly arranging and adding to the mix. The older boy watched with silent interest, while the younger one picked up a panel from the stack, walked to Kmetra and held it out.

Maisie kept an eye out as Kmetra suppressed a smile, gently

taking the painting from him and placing it a few meters away. Returning to the pile with him, she grabbed the top panel and handed it over, pointing to his chest. She did the same with the older boy, then pointed again, into the distance.

"Time to go, boys," Maisie said quietly, tilting her head in the direction of the fields they came from. The boys hesitated, watching as Kmetra returned to work. After a minute, they lost interest and ran, chasing each other, kicking up dust and flinging their paintings into the air, watching them twirl and running to the spots where they landed.

Kmetra distributed the remaining panels in and around the perimeter, then seemed to lose focus. She absent–mindedly pulled out clumps of grass and let them fall in the breeze. "Time to go, yeh?" Maisie urged impatiently, eyeing the silhouette of a bat hawk against the crepuscular backdrop.

***

As the blue hour sank into night, the paintings subtly emitted their own light. The muted colors transformed into fluorescent, vividly glowing geometries, appearing to absorb the fading color of the earth and dusk air. The relative emptiness was broken by the sound of field crickets and nocturnal animals rustling to action. Then, later, the sound of distant voices, carried by the breeze.

"...Off the grounds." Crawford looked down his pointed nose at Maisie with a cold gaze, leaning to one side in his chair. The early morning sunlight caught his white hair and a segment of archaeological books on the far wall.

Maisie sat in business attire on the opposite side of his austere desk. "You know I believe in what you're doing here," she said respectfully after a pause, "I did what I felt was in line with that, and helpful to her, even though..."

"Our philosophy is not ambiguous when it comes to tangency," Crawford countered, "...*Especially* in a situation like this." A long moment passed. He shifted forward, his movement spry for nearly eighty. "Do you suppose," he said, narrowing sharp blue eyes between crows' feet, "there's a chance she caught sight of anything?"

"No," she responded soberly, "not a chance."

Crawford's eyes drifted to the Chilean pine in the far corner, lost in thought. After a deep breath, he said "I'm relieving you of your responsibilities to Kmetra, and putting you in charge of Milles."

Maisie's eyes widened as she subtly straightened in her chair. "Oh, I can't do that!"

"You can't do that?!" He looked at her incredulously, "Do you realize how many messages I've received in the last twelve hours?"

He gestured toward his desk. "I have members of the press calling me, the board, this person or that person, *every minute*. Her life is forever altered. I can't just put a lid on this and carry on," he said, miming a brush off with his hand, "as much as I'd like that. I don't want to spend one second longer than necessary dealing with this, but it demands my focus for a while."

Maisie stared at the grasslands out the window, biting her tongue. "Listen," he continued, his tone softening, "this is not a form of punishment. I need your help. You'll never go in there alone, nor should you." Maisie nodded abruptly.

"Look on the bright side," he said dryly, "At least you know he's not going to take off on you."

"I don't calibrate here though," Koji answered in heavily accented English, "Three months contract." The windowless walls absorbed his gruff voice, a strangely anechoic semicircular chamber with a half dozen large padded chairs angled toward a desk between two narrow doors. Jiǎnhuàzì text accompanied subtly playful emergency exit maps. Fresnel vents ran in disjointed lines down the curved wall, channeling the ambient gold of afternoon sun as the sole light source. "Many experiments on the signal data," Koji continued, "lot of unsolved problems."

John listened actively, a stray sunbeam highlighting his pale olive complexion. "Any other leads from the public domain?" He asked casually, before the sound of a door opening and the chatter of a woman giving inaudible parting orders to a silent colleague.

The men stood as Chantal entered, greeting Koji with a crisp handshake as he gave a stilted half–bow and straightened his tie. Chantal's hair was pinned back in a goethite clasp, her dark twill–weave suit jacket covering the subtle mosaic of a cross–patterned silk blouse. She and John exchanged a quick smile and shook hands. "Make yourselves comfortable," she urged before sitting on the corner of the desk as they returned to where they were.

"I trust you've both seen the news today?" The men nodded.

"Well, our press officer has been fielding some inquiries. Our official response so far has been 'no comment.' However, I think it would be smart for you to have a cursory look into this."

John looked at her with befuddled amusement, turning his palms upward. "Any particular reason?" he asked flatly, "I mean, look into what? UNEXA isn't in the habit of debunking hoaxes."

"No, it isn't," she agreed as Koji stood and began pacing the sandstone–textured floor, "But I've seen some additional details and I'm obligated to exercise due diligence, before issuing a statement."

"You have information the press doesn't?" Koji touched his thumb and middle finger in the air as he walked.

"Maybe not. Obscure connections no one's reported yet, if they found them," she waited a beat before continuing.

"The institution where this woman lives has minimal public records," Chantal went on, "but the gentleman who runs it publishes numerous papers. They're peer–reviewed and well respected."

"Research?" John probed as Koji listened, walking in a slow figure eight.

"At a glance, it's Byzantine, specialized academia; '*idiosyncratic semiotics.*' It's nearly opaque to me. But he makes some… *references*, that suggest there's more to see."

Koji stared upward, peering into the ivy covering the ceiling. "Sounds like substantial diversion."

"Not really," Chantal resisted the notion with a smile, "We've messaged the institution, and located a relief photographer in the vicinity, one of our contractors… well, he's in Khartoum. Still early in the morning there. Anyway, certainly he's closer than we are," she stood to leave.

"Well, this'll give me a chance to hassle Koji about his exploits," John said, relaxing in his chair a bit and giving a wide grin to his restless partner.

"Yes, I'm sure you know Mr. Kurita by reputation, but knowing him personally is something else entirely," she winked in Koji's direction, her Mesoamerican accent surfacing as she acquainted them. "John's particularly good at getting problems unstuck. He's a great lateral thinker, with a very abstract, angular approach. We frequently put unusual results or anomalous data in front of him."

Koji nodded, looking relieved, the light temperature subtly cooling beneath a rapidly moving cloud.

Midday poured in through the corridor's high glass ceiling, fixed partway up adobe–hued walls. Maisie listened intently, keeping pace with Adjetey as they walked. "Don't touch the cage under any circumstances," he said softly but sternly.

"Stay within two meters of me at all times. When I unlock the inner door, stay directly behind me until it's been locked again," he loped ahead of her, steady and deliberate.

Maisie's gaze drifted to a faded laser–scar, barely visible, inside his right ear. "Adjetey?"

He turned to face her directly, passing an alcove with a lancet arch. A small olive tree inside took respite from the peak sun.

"He doesn't know about the connection. And, for the moment…"

Adjetey smiled and pointed to his skull. "You're in charge of everything up here."

They had reached a reinforced door of petrified wood. He rifled through his keys.

"Adjetey…" Maisie repeated more quietly as his ear cocked to listen, "Have you ever been in here with a woman?"

"I've accompanied Dr. Saxo on numerous occasions," he hesitated, his expression increasingly focused as he unlocked the outer door. Maisie's flashed apprehension, inhaling sharply through her teeth before morphing into resolve.

The petrified wood slid sideways with a loud clank. More daylight greeted them as they stepped into a dirt floored cage of diamond–meshed wire. Rectangular and narrow, three meters wide and high, the enclosure served as an entryway to a massive twenty by thirty meter space. Maisie looked beyond their reinforced iron frame as Adjetey locked them in.

To the right, uneven, slightly rolling earth held a thick grove of mostly baobab trees. The floor beneath was collaged with ancient Devonian seed ferns, taro, and myriad vegetation. Adjetey scanned the inner landscape cautiously, from the tops of the trees down to the far corners. Birdsong was audible, but no birds were visible.

A moment passed before Adjetey turned to Maisie and nodded subtly. He efficiently moved left, opening the inner door and slipping in with her as she held her breath. They stood in the far corner of the room as he locked them in, their immediate surrounding a mini–landscape of dirt and pebbles.

High overhead, long transparent panes of greenhouse glass angled to a central peak, held by a delicate gray–white metal framing.

"Milles!" Adjetey called out. Nothing but the singing of invisible birds. The bright sunlight caught dust particles in the air. Wary, he started to walk slowly toward the trees, Maisie following obediently as they avoided a broad pile of sticks and branches.

The dense grove provided shade as they weaved inside, the walls nearly disappearing. A long half–minute passed. The ground became wet and moss covered, silencing their footsteps.

Maisie heard the cracking of a branch above. A blurred figure landed on Adjetey's shoulders as he lurched sideways, pinning Milles underneath his back. They exchanged blows immediately, pummeling each other and defending body and face shots. Maisie jumped clear as they tumbled, Milles gaining the upper hand for a few seconds before Adjetey twisted and rolled. He grabbed Milles' sleeve as he tried to stand, then charged into him from the ground, knocking his opponent into the clearing as he barreled after him.

The fight continued, a standing brawl for a brief moment. Adjetey's cropped hair was too short to grab, but Milles wrenched at his collar, dragging him to the ground where his size and weight were less relevant.

The two men writhed and threw dust in the air for the nearly a minute, each taking a bruising, before Adjetey scrambled to pin him in a groundfighting hold. Milles gasped a bit as he struggled, losing his breath but getting a few face shots that Adjetey took with remarkable endurance.

"*Had enough?!*" Milles spat in defiance, staring deep into Adjetey's face and breathing hard through his nose. Maisie descended from the trees, having kept more distance than she was told.

Adjetey released him and stood straight, dusting himself as Milles gradually rose to his feet. He took a wide bowlegged stance in blue coveralls, scarred hands on his knees.

"Not bad, that time," Adjetey offered, probing his mouth with a ring finger.

"Fuck you." Milles spat light pink again before his eyes darted away, scrutinizing Maisie.

"I'm Maisie Blanca," she stared back into his bearded scowl, her face a mask of steel nerves.

"Where's Crawford?"

"He has other business at the moment," Adjetey replied.

"Dr. Saxo," Milles deadpanned, "is a fucking coward." His gravelly voice filled the room as he stood upright.

"How are you feeling, Milles?" Maisie asked with gentle affect.

"Like a polished diamond," he replied, beaming sincerely for a moment. "Get to the point, what's this parade for? You hungry for some abuse?" He licked his teeth.

"We're here to get an update on your work," Maisie answered evenly, "and also to ask you a favor." She gazed upward. Along the top of the room's dark gray concrete walls was a collection of Kmetra's paintings. Perhaps two hundred panels in muted colors, stacked three high to form a patchwork border ten meters above, between the concrete and the transparent roof. "We'd like to have Uncle Sasha bring in a photographer tomorrow to archive your paintings."

Milles raised his eyebrows and chuckled, before breaking his gaze and looking for something. "Ego strokes are no good in here," He glanced at Adjetey, who stood with arms crossed, before returning to Maisie. "You all owe me a litany of favors anyway."

Maisie turned to Adjetey, who shook his head. "No one outside this greenhouse would say that," his voice low and steady.

"You don't have any *honor*, man! You're gonna ignore what I said. At least Kmetra knows what *loyalty* is."

"...Uh, I'm a little confused," Maisie said, discomfort creeping into her voice.

"No, you're not," Milles retaliated, uncomfortably close as his voice raised to a shout, "You know what you'd have without me? *Fucking picnics on the moon*!"

Adjetey swiftly moved between them, filling Milles' line of sight in a brutal stance.

Crawford's hands folded on top of the table, which illuminated with regularity between them. "Why not just use the Vinča signal?" He leaned back.

Eric pondered a response. "Charley feels this would be... closer to the spirit of the company, rather than the signal itself," his voice was slightly tense, but pleasant and articulate, "Besides, it's impossible to secure an exclusive license for private use." He brushed unseen dust from an immaculate three piece cotton suit. "You're legally responsible for her?"

"She's a ward of the institute," Crawford responded. Out the window behind him, a sudden breeze rippled across the grasses, the antique soda–lime glass warping the movement. "I appreciate your visit, but unfortunately this isn't the sort of funding I'd imagined from our correspondence."

Eric leaned forward and reached beside his chair, "...You might find the financial aspect to be greater than you had imagined." Crawford opened a resisting hand. "Frankly, this kind of exposure isn't good for Kmetra, or for the institute."

Eric smiled, his features softening. "You know I've never met my boss? I'm probably as closely associated to Charley as anyone you're liable to see in public. Hermetically sealed and globally connected is a contradiction we embrace," he paused, "and we're the best at it."

"I'm sure being globally connected works out well in your case," Crawford returned a polite smile, "In spite of the events that brought you here, it's counter–productive for us."

"How did it happen, anyway?"

Crawford said nothing, silence filling the gap.

"Perhaps it's possible that she wants to expand beyond the walls here?" Eric offered.

"Kmetra's motivations," Crawford's eyes winced lightly, "are not easily discerned."

Eric smiled again, reaching gently for a bronze–rimmed espresso cup. "Well as you can imagine, my boss is not easily deterred."

***

The pinhole sized light flashed on the graphite door before it slid sideways. Kmetra retained focus on a panel in the corner, painting deliberately with a matted brush, squatting amongst a scattered collection of tubes littered across the floor.

Crawford entered first, followed by a rail thin young man with a perfect quiff of auburn hair.

"Good morning Kmetra. This is Mr. Pressman," Crawford introduced them politely.

"Hello Kmetra," Eric observed her work while Crawford dug into his pocket and produced a bill of burnt–orange rag paper, covered with interference patterns and a thin copper stripe.

He handed it to Eric. "We still use paper currency out here," he said, tilting his head subtly toward the painter in the corner.

A sole windowpane, slovenly covered in translucent red, cast a tint on Kmetra's saturnine features. Her dark skin reflected an almost blue hue, highlighting the contours of her slender face. Overhead, more daylight flooded in through mackerel clouds and the modest room's glass top.

Eric stepped over and leaned in, presenting the note to Kmetra with an eerily crisp perfection of movement.

Kmetra's eyes darted sideways, and she turned to look at him. Deep brown eyes, indistinguishable pupils. She looked down at his offering, gingerly pinching it with an inscrutable expression.

Looking back to her work, the currency found fresh paint as she pressed it firmly into the panel. She quickly swept a brush over it in decisive motion, securing it at a peculiar angle before continuing where she'd left off.

Crawford stifled a laugh. "Haven't seen that one yet," he said, walking into her kitchen area. A triad of miniature fruit trees sat in a ceramic tile box, two cubic meters of moist earth beneath them. A series of organic, vascular green pads nestled against hexagonal fresnel vents, smothered bright white highlights in the cool shade.

"She gets her basic, like everyone else," he picked a crimson clementine and started peeling it, "we take deliveries of things she seems interested in." He ate a slice, tossing bits of rind into a square compost recess in the tilework. "If she understands the principle of money, I've never seen any acknowledgment of it."

"Well, it would be careless of me to leave without at least presenting a contract to you," Eric pressed three fingers to the nearest wall in a conspicuous hand gesture.

Crawford scratched his forehead. "We don't have living walls in here. Kmetra painted on them," he gestured toward the pile of blank panels in an opposing corner of the room, their color and texture perfectly matching the surrounding structure.

Eric reached into a razor thin briefcase and pulled out a thin slab, which illuminated as he passed it over. Kmetra's attention diverted from the painting once more, curiously staring over the tablet. "She seems interested."

"Yes she has an affinity for illumined objects," Crawford responded absent–mindedly, his eyes scanning the text.

Eric squatted down to inspect the work more closely, staring into her rather expensive collage.

"…What sort of twenty first century contract is this?" Crawford suddenly looked offended, "*'in perpetuity throughout the universe'*?"

"Dr. Saxo, this seems… different. It doesn't look like the work I've seen before."

Rows of heavily scratched redwood planks filtered chalk stripes of light into the barren concrete bunker. Milles kneeled on tea–colored sheets over thick, long strips of Japanese maple, cut raw, bark intact on the top side. A sharp metallic object ricocheted stray photons as he aggressively scraped a long groove. He lifted a heavy object, grunting as the sound of hammering and splintering rang against the walls.

Subvocal murmurs accompanied the rustling wooden clack of rearrangement. A menacing yowl, with fragments of a degrading narrative. The sound of aggravation, and a clear "I *warned* you," as the hammer and metal returned, violently pushing bark into a fresh curve, revealing naked tree flesh.

***

A young Lobi man, not yet twenty, used a rope–and–pulley to slide the titanium scaffolding in short bursts over the din of birds and Milles' chiseling. Nearly ten meters up, the relief photographer braced himself against the railing with one hand, perilously securing his equipment with the other. "Good!" he called out. Uncle Sasha locked a mechanism into place. He released the rope, leaning against the wall before languidly removing his gloves.

The photographer wiped away sweat, the hot glass roof close enough to touch as he repositioned his tripod, leveling a multi–lensed black felt box. A series of guttural shouts caused him to peer anxiously into the baobab thicket below. In the farthest corner, menacing mutterings caused his eyes to widen, but he saw no one. He glanced down at Uncle Sasha, who stared in the direction of the sun with his eyes closed.

Taking a moment and a tense breath, he returned to his focus, Kmetra's flatly–lit paintings filling the camera's prismatic inner geometry.

A single panel filled the screen to the bleeding edge, floor to ceiling, nine times larger than life. The outsized brush strokes brutally formed ochre shapes of notched brick, mixed with rectilinear orpiment and vermilion shreds, abruptly broken crimson stripes, interlocking hexagonal bits of white scattered in one corner.

The image gave fresh color and perspective to the room, a bone colored scalene triangle with two Chinese elms twisting out of its most acute angle.

John stood off center, poring over the details on screen with his chin resting in his hand. "Any layers underneath these?"

"Infrequent," Koji replied from a womb chair near the door in the opposite corner, "images could be changed later to match."

"Or test colors," John said, eyes not diverting, "is there any way to date them?"

Koji shook his head even though neither looked at each other. "Dries very quickly. No sun damage." John flipped through to another with a brief hand movement.

"What kind of paint is this?" John pressed on.

"All mass market. Nothing special. Some colors, phosphorous acrylic resin. Some, water based phosphor and synthetic egg."

"Anything else in here?"

"Yes. Strands of dog hair. *Lycaon pictus.*"

"So someone's making her own brushes," John gazed, the images flipping by.

Koji exhaled and leaned forward, his charcoal business attire covering the slab in his lap. He cupped his face in his hands, talking through his fingers. "I can't believe how much time I lose to this. Ridiculous."

John doubled over in laughter, his tie dangling. Koji looked over with a begrudging half smile. "This is a normal afternoon for you?"

John regained his composure and cleared his throat. "Sort of. I haven't seen my desk for weeks," he wiped his face, "...You find anything in the research papers?"

"Nothing conclusive."

John walked to the chair as Koji handed the slab to John. After a moment, the Cantonese characters became Latin. John scratched the back of his head as he scanned the material.

"Okay," he said suddenly, walking to far corner of the room and tossing the slab behind the elms, clattering against a clay pot, "Let's have a thought experiment."

The tree leaves brushed gently against the ceiling. John closed the lights as a subtle breeze behind them came to a standstill on his command, giving the space an unnatural silence.

The room's inky blackness was penetrated immediately by dilating pupils and the phosphorescent pigment on screen. Its muted forms became vivid fluorescent red, yellow, hot pink, white and electric blue, a rectangular alien jellyfish as bright as the moon.

Koji got up from his chair as John leaned his head against the screen wall and closed one eye, looking along the low mountainous relief. He twisted one hand against the cool surface as the other dragged three fingers inward. The topography of the painting extended outward into the room, filling the entire angled space with distorted holographic hills and valleys.

The giant light sculpture reflected in Koji's dark brown eyes. It glitched and reflected stray slivers of image as he wandered into it, brush strokes appearing like sweeping cliff faces.

"Low res," Koji noted, staring upward and casting a hand back and forth. Several sections degraded into harsh chunks of visible polygons, jittering as they struggled to find their orientation.

"Let's just assume for a moment that the timing is accurate," John walked toward Koji through the image, throwing a shapeshifting shadow on the walls, "The first mention of her in the research is over two years old."

"I suppose is a consideration. If this woman has wormhole in her brain," Koji said softly as he paced inside the media, making a gesture like he held a sphere, "Is a beautiful thought."

John flipped through a few images, various colors and distended shapes flickering over them. "Is there anything mathematically significant in the other sixty percent?"

"Inexplicable, random."

"Aesthetically fluid though. I can't tell them apart," John peered into the exaggerated contours, "Does it look to you like they were created in a frenzy?"

Koji nodded. "Would need to be."

"I agree it looks like fast work. But it also looks very deliberate to me. Directional. Not a lot of hesitation."

Koji reflected bizarre ripples as he walked over to the wall and touched lightly. The painting snapped back into two dimensions, emptying the room in an instant. "Anyone making so many in seventy hours would be fast and precise."

Uncle Sasha rode in the passenger cab of the delivery transport, the dim sound of low frequency counterpoint bass ending abruptly as it arrived at the northwest side of the residence. Around the corner, Maisie emerged from an ogee–arched double doorway, pushing a metal dolly over the grass.

"I have it," Sasha assured in his Francophone accent, casually gripping the handles of a crate. She maneuvered to the red dirt path and locked the wheels in place. His toned forearms flexed and relaxed. "Not much today."

She nodded, squinting as she strained to see in the mid–afternoon sun. Her eyes fixed on a patch of shade on the side of the building, where something caught her focus.

She walked over to a tall corrugated recycling skip, peering over the ledge. A crumple of smoky translucent plastic. A splayed stack of spectral acetate sheets in myriad colors.

Sasha snapped the wheel lock free and rolled his payload toward the back door. The transport pulled away, driverless, playing music to an empty cab as it picked up speed.

Maisie grabbed a protruding Sudano–Sahelian beam and hoisted herself up the outer wall for better access. She lifted the plastic aside, revealing an overturned, intricately folded piece of titanium furniture and several dozen thin, transparent perspelx panels.

A gust of harmattan wind caught the wrapping before she pinned it with quick reflexes. A paper card flailed back and forth:

To Kmetra
A gift. with best wishes for your future
—Charley
utere fexix

***

"Dr. Saxo," She opened the screen door forcefully, startling a family of African crakes, krr–ing and running. Bird calls travelled in all directions. A vast glass enclosure curved away from the almost fifty meter long concrete inner wall, meeting the dirt and a stream thirty meters out. The water passed through a low iron grate, organically bisecting the space before winding into a tunnel near the far wall.

Crawford stood in mismatched browns, textile weaves clashing. He pruned the low branches of a doka by the creek. A swamp hen stood by, pecking twigs with a red beak as they fell to the ground.

Maisie stepped across a clapper bridge and held out the card. Crawford looked over briefly. "Digging through the trash?" A snapping sound as another twig fell.

"What is this?" Maisie had a perplexed look on her face.

"From Mr. Pressman, a young gentleman who came by last week," Crawford began to explain, "I think he may have been *g–m*, but I didn't want to be rude. He wanted to buy Kmetra's work for the identity of his employer."

"*utere fexix*?" Maisie uttered in disbelief, "I guess you have no idea who they are…" She pinched the fabric of her blouse with pale fingers.

"Well he presented an absurd contract," Crawford walked to a locust bean tree and inspected the low–hanging branches, "Not that it makes any difference."

Maisie's expression was bewildered. "Doctor, you know I think you're a brilliant man," she said, "But you are also a *fool*."

A covey of blue quail flew low across the ground from a thicket of nearby shrubbery as Crawford tossed the shears onto moss and turned to face her. "I just got done cleaning up the mess you helped to make."

"You're enjoying your gardening?" Maisie opened her arms.

"Not a moment's rest," his face fell wearily, "What makes you so sure this 'gift' isn't a negotiation?"

"Unless there's a contract buried in the skip?" she indicated outside, "I dare say they have a better understanding of what we do around here than you right now."

"You're not putting that in her quarters," his voice was firm.

Maisie shook her head and pointed. "Right here. No one says a word to anyone. Including her." She slid the card into her pocket.

Crawford's reluctant expression lingered for a long moment.

"Sasha!" Maisie called to the door.

***

The sun set beyond the glass into the expanse of desert–savannah. Birds settled as the rich blue of nautical twilight filled the aviary.

Kmetra's features caught the table's backlight as she folded a crease into a magenta sheet and tore a rhombic fragment with manic energy. She worked furiously, mixing crystalline dye with water from the stream and wiping the gel across the glowing perspelx, which flash dried in place after a few seconds.

A black stork warily ambled past on stick legs. For a moment, the sky and the light of the table mirrored an iridescent purple. Kmetra slid the finished work aside, exposing bright white as she loaded a new panel, then introduced fresh color as she mixed and folded in the dark.

"...[*inaudible*] background radiation–"

The boxwood door clattered open and shut, treble frequencies amplified by hard surfaces. Floor to ceiling glass on the opposite wall permitted the open shade of overcast sky. Chantal's silhouette was softened by a skylight over her wide desk. Giant succulents thrust upward on both sides from pebble lined openings in nephrite tile.

Koji stood opposite her, mid–sentence, one hand gripping the back of a chair. John offered a succinct apology as he walked briskly to the vacant seat. Chantal nodded as Koji touched a forefinger to his eyebrow.

"I'm trying to make sense of a controversial point in your brief," Chantal's Harris tweed blazer caught the artificial glow of her desk. "Mr. Kurita seems eager to sweep it under the rug."

John nodded, suppressing a smile. "That's quite linear of him," he opined as Koji's fingers drummed the back of an empty chair.

"Is the conclusion in dispute?" Chantal's question lingered as John took a moment.

"Well, let's say I accept its ambiguity."

"Very oblique," Koji replied. He started pacing the floor, his hand conducting an unseen orchestra.

John leaned back. "You know the public version of the Vinča signal is a raw, unedited recording. One iteration of the loop, including some static noise and interference. However, two paintings photographed at the institute match the internal, compiled master signal. Data that's obscured in the public domain."

"Very lucky guess, most likely." Koji wandered to the window, peering down a cliff through distant oxidized metalwork into the sinkhole below. A half–kilometer dish, formed by thousands of triangular segments, held off the advance of surrounding forest. Across neighboring mountaintops, jagged corners of pristine limestone buildings and irregular black glass windows formed a broken circumference. The sweeping high altitude ring of sharply interconnecting shapes merged silently into the earth. "Would be extraordinary, if provable."

"This woman and the institute hasn't exactly been relishing the attention," John continued, "Not a peep. Not one scrap of media."

"That works in our favor for the moment," Chantal noted, pausing as Koji returned to his chair. "They've also been very accommodating to our requests. Nevertheless, it's secondhand information. Our agency has higher priorities than waiting for a motive to crystallize."

"We recommend to close the file," Koji suggested politely after a moment. "No statement."

She took a few seconds of her own to think. Her desk flickered. "What guarantee do I have that your conclusion is future–proof?" Snake plant and aloe ferox hovered nearby. The men exchanged glances.

"…We do have an idea for that."

Steam rose from boiling water, splashing flecks refracting incandescent light on rustic blue tesserae. Field crickets sang from a cracked open window. The rustle of Xaya's pencil on the kitchen table stopped.

Crawford rubbed an eye. "Something black. I have a late call with the board."

She murmured in recollection. Her ringed hand dipped into a row of jars, tossing dried leaves into the bubbling carafe. "…Your work is extraordinary, you know that."

He looked into the floor. "Kmetra's been at it for weeks. Definitely different now… I think I'm losing it." His low voice trailed off.

"Mmm," her smile revealed deep wrinkles as she gave his arm a tender rub, "This won't stop with you. It was never the plan to keep the lid on forever, was it?"

He shrugged, watching the drifting particles darken the water.

***

"Uncle Sasha was listening to the signal on the grounds the day of Kmetra's… outing." Megateo listened to Crawford from a wide screen nestled in a wall of books. A few gaps in the shelves held glass–enclosed primitive clay objects, textile effigies, and a large quartz fragment with glyphs carved in relief. "If she recognized the *sound*, that would certainly make things more interesting."

Teo's smile was big. "What's the opinion of UNEXA?"

"They're about as skeptical as I suppose I would be. I'm getting ready to send them the first batch of images of her latest work, if the board approves their request..."

"Of course! It's a big, incredible mystery. Really fantastic."

"You seem quite comfortable with it all." Crawford sank into his leather club chair, reaching for a square tea glass on the adjacent reading table.

"Why to be uncomfortable?" His Chilean–hued English skewed his grammar. He waited a beat, his question unanswered. "...You know what I love about being nearly one hundred?"

Confounded, Crawford lifted a hand from the armchair, palm inward. "That you're still alive?"

Teo's laughter was loud enough to wake Xaya, who stirred in the next room. "It's a gift," he smiled, "but also, I love to make everyone around me feel young. Even *you*."

Crawford's countenance lightened a little.

"Speaking of young persons. What about the identity? What do you think these days?" The late afternoon light streaming from Teo's window contrasted sharply with the midnight darkness of the study.

Crawford sighed. "Another subject I'm reluctant to discuss."

Teo's exuberance was undeterred. "The decision is up to you. The board is behind you. You *invented* this field," he continued, "We trust your judgment."

A few seconds of silence as Crawford quietly nodded, lost in thought.

"Hey," Teo said slyly, clapping his hands as if to clear the mood. "I have some news guaranteed to cheer you up a bit. We may have a candidate for you."

"A new resident?" Crawford's eyes opened wider.

"Sí. The board reviews it now, Alma and Omar are having a look, give their recommendation, and if it's positive..."

"Anything you can tell me?"

Teo offered another large smile, "It's fair to say that you will have no trouble recognizing this person on arrival."

"*Now arriving in New Quahigoya,*" A disembodied voice quietly chimed in the cab. Crawford's neck craned sideways, looking out the curved window. A haze of swirling dust shrouded the view as he rode through the outskirts, past sand covered streets and battered store fronts. Brief glimpses of pedestrians in colorful tagelmusts, a group of children struggling to play kickball, small flocks of red-necked ostriches tucked into narrow alleys.

The cab meshed effortlessly into slowing street traffic as buildings became taller, more dense, climbing into metropolitan skyscrapers. "Somewhere around here," Crawford said aloud to no one. The voice chimed again softly in Tamazight and French, pulling to a curb.

Crawford braced himself, ducking into the khamsin wind. Immediately pelted with airborne sand, he held his scarf as a makeshift veil as he walked haltingly to a covered sidewalk and through a wide door a few steps below street level.

***

Dim light and a maze of horseshoe arches divided several cavernous chambers filled with tables and the din of conversation and music. Exquisite art deco carpets and interior details blended seamlessly with Moorish architecture. Eric and Crawford sat in a secluded corner.

"Will you join me in a *pito*?" Eric asked as they neared the end of their meal.

Crawford placed a sterling fork on the china and dabbed his mouth with a napkin. "Let me have a last look," he said, swallowing his bite, "I'll probably need one afterward."

Eric smiled tightly as he handed the slate over from its case. "A brief medical checkup is all we've added. A standard insurance."

"Your people?"

"Yes."

"No press requirements?" Crawford's eyes darted down the text.

"What are we going to do? Grant interviews?" Eric bluntly joked. "Kmetra will have the same relationship to the press that Charley does," he assured, "which is none at all."

A waiter came by to collect the dishes. Eric engaged him in a brief conversation in French, before continuing. "Your institute will also have access to experimental products during the license period, if you wish."

"I'm sure Maisie will be happy to hear that," Crawford stopped reading and looked over the table sternly. "I still have reservations about this. I'll be beyond upset if Kmetra's situation worsens."

"I won't pretend that there is no risk whatsoever to what you do. Or what I think you do..." Eric reasoned, his tone crisp and uncanny, "but we're uniquely suited to cater to the needs of a prominent recluse–"

The waiter reappeared with two glasses of *pito*, and a crumber swept across the tablecloth. Eric exhaled in relief, as they raised their glasses to toast.

"The dust storm is expected to settle this afternoon," he suggested with a half smile as he sipped.

Kmetra emerged first, slowly pushing a loaded cart through a wide entryway and rolling her spectral cargo down the embankment toward a transport. The sun touched the treetops and caught the floral engraving on the ebony doors. Maisie shut and locked the main entrance next to a small bronze plaque: *Institut de Recherche pour Idiosyncrasiques Sémiotique.*

She hastily caught up, overtook Kmetra and opened the side door. They disappeared inside the cab with a collective hoist, sitting opposite each other, Maisie next to a narrow opening at the front. Locked in the middle was a series of bright perspelx abstractions, nearly a hundred vertically stacked and held fast in a borrowed crate.

Maisie sat quietly, arms half folded, her blouse of patchwork rayon and kente holding an argent brooch. Kmetra stared over the gallery forest as they accelerated alongside it, pupils darting rapidly back and forth.

The transport cast a long shadow over grassland and savannah. In the far distance ahead, a series of connected transport cars barreled down an orange path through the ecotone.

***

The delivery transport rode quietly onto the grounds of the

institute just after sunset, shutting down in the grass about twenty meters out. Inside the passenger cab, Uncle Sasha made himself more comfortable as the lights flickered off, leaving the faint yellow glow of the instrument panels and the buzzing rattle of an intense gyil performance emanating from the interior. He stretched out on the bench seat, closing his eyes below a side window as the eastern sky slowly bled a deep blue.

Inside the sealed cargo area, a vague figure lay nestled between boxes, illuminated only by dim green safety light. A masquerade–style covering of partially dried hair grass and infrequent strips of loose plastic covered the figure from head to toe in a complex weave, making it difficult to determine the contours of the body beneath. A mask of bird feathers formed a wooly, faceless head, disproportionately tall, a sculptural black and brown plumage on white, its subtly abstract facial features blending indiscriminately into the oversized body below it.

***

The transport approached the train, decelerating as it closed the gap between them. Dust kicked up under the bouncing tires, then a mechanical, magnetic clack. Kmetra reached out to steady herself as the momentum of the train overtook the car.

Maisie pointed three closed fingers toward her mouth, then pointed toward the opening to her left. "I'll be right back." She tapped a panel and the opening slid into a passage. She greeted unseen passengers in the next car, as the passage slid shut again.

Kmetra turned to the opposite opening beside her, touching an identical panel. A rush of loud air and a flurry of dust. She stood, grasping handles at either end as she stepped out onto the gangway, watching the rush of road erupt beneath her in loud streaks.

She reached for black service rungs on the outer body of the car, swinging nimbly as she climbed a few feet. Her face caught the draft over the car's curved top, blowing her hood to her shoulders and undoing a knot of cornrows, half of them streaming behind her wildly as she stood tall in the wind.

The road sank lower, beneath the surroundings. Kmetra ducked down just before the opening to a subterranean tunnel barely cleared the top of the cars. She crouched, fetal, her stygian robes rippling on eggshell white as they plunged into darkness, red sunlight disappearing behind her in a rapidly shrinking circle, the tunnel wind a claustrophobic howl.

The blackness was pierced by a sidelong row of tiny lights. Kmetra fixed her eyes on them as they began to animate. As if inside a zoetrope, the lights grew into land forms and countries, a map tracing the train's northern route, text flashing through half a dozen languages, followed by a flurry of advertisements.

***

A jerky rotation of its head, and a rustle as the figure's rough shapes began to turn and move through the crate stacks in a ritualistic fashion. Two arms with a hundred grassy blade–fingers pressed against the inside of the door. It clicked, gliding sideways as the figure darted out, crouching and swerving. The grating sibilation of the gyil's song was muffled, but audible as Sasha rested invisibly in the cab.

A rustling shake of its arms, and it moved again, swiveling its head and shaking in a low and threatening dance–like gesture, before disappearing into tall Rhodesian bluegrass. After a few seconds, it emerged again, slowly making its way in a stop–and–start zigzag toward the treeline at the edge of the grounds.

The breeze rippled the vegetation in waves as the grassy figure moved with the grain of the landscape surrounding it. Eventually it blurred as it moved deeper into the trees, becoming indistinguishable from the dense foliage as the day faded into purple twilight.

***

Maisie and Kmetra's transport gently disconnected from cars at either end as the train crept slowly through a New Qua station, the cab swiftly angling into a space under the pedestrian platform.

Kmetra pushed her cart in a slow shuffle up the moving walkway. The dark sky overhead was framed by glass buildings, caked with sand. Their golden interior light spilled into the street, the innards alive with human activity. Dirty neon signs flashed rainbows of color, dancing off of acetate shards and glinting through her paintings.

A few passers–by paused to stare as they rose to street level. Most hurriedly moved around Kmetra's cart on their way elsewhere as she looked upward, Maisie standing a few paces behind her.

Down the straight cobblestone road, amidst an array of giant structures dotted with squeaky clean panels, was an obsidian skyscraper, a colossal obelisk merging with a stepped series of aerodynamically rounded rectangles. Without a spec of dust, it seemed to absorb everything and reflect nothing, giving the appearance a piece of the city was missing.

Maisie looked over Kmetra's shoulder. On a street corner in the near distance stood two well dressed figures: Dr. Saxo and Mr. Pressman.

***

Sasha drifted off under the purple–black sky and the first twinkling stars of dusk. The gyil concert had faded into the calls of night mammals, crickets, and wind in leaves. The cargo door hung open.

In the far corner of the residence, a rusted staircase of perforated aluminum spiraled up to a mesh landing bolted to a concrete wall. A sole incandescent bulb shone through a wire door, a mammoth curved glass ceiling protruding just above it.

At the edge of the light, the grassy figure reappeared and dropped to one knee, both hands to the earth. In similar chaotic motion, it approached the rusty metal helix in a low crouch, rash and deliberate, winding its way up as impressionistic eyeless faces rotated in its plumage.

The figure opened the wire door, slowly entering the cagey hallway, followed by the squeaking hinges of the inner door. Its shadow disappeared as a kāmaʻo flew out of the aviary, its brown feathers blurring in the light.

[3 years later]

Euclidean tiles of blistering manganese violet, manifolds of flat black, mother–of–pearl iridescent broken beaks and cavernous polygonal trenches synchronized with the sound of clicking beetles packed in corrugated silica.

Crinkled static and a flickering sequence of sharp mercurial kites preceded a meteoric blaze of magenta razors and phlox purple polyforms, concave quadrilaterals and frozen splinters of fluorescent red, microseconds of choir–like snippets arranged with infinitely spliced magnetic tape, acid etched leaves scraping asphalt.

Dissonant harmonics resonated over cyan and seagreen smears cut into crystalline hematite, semigraphic structures in flat trigonal silhouette.

Almost two hundred seconds of media faded into Gaussian–like dust in kilobit color, the sound of a distant collapsing snowdrift expanding into a bone–crunching tidal wave swept beneath human hearing.

A half second of low, sub–bass hum signaled a final scorching series of contact sparks, overblown glitches of blue noise and flash–blinding amber white vertical splinters, blinking millisecond white and then black.

$$\alpha\ 03^{\text{h}}\ 27^{\text{m}}\ 59.7^{\text{s}}$$
$$\delta\ \text{-}73°\ 16'\ 25''$$

Runoff trickled through rain gutters, dripping arrhythmically onto tin ventilation shafts. John placed both hands on a damp ledge and looked up. A quarter moon high overhead was mostly covered by dark drifting clouds, crisp stars between the linings despite the lunar disturbance and bright skyline at the horizon. A textless, ten meter billboard towered far behind him, tiled to the bleed line with jaggedly colored backlit perspelx extending the length of the roof.

He looked down the high building's slick black glass to the rush of street noise far below. His tie waved in the breeze, partially concealing a view of a block–long Whitney umbrella: a bizarre frozen twist of illogical colors in the same glowing palette as the billboard, suspended several stories above street level with the support of the opposite building.

At the gentle slam of the service hatch, he turned his head. For a moment, he saw nothing except the distorted reflections of magenta and red in motionless rain puddles, moonlight on wet tarpaper, and silhouettes of industrial machinery. Along an adjacent wall, Koji appeared from behind a cooling unit.

"My old friend!" John embraced him before grabbing the collar of his rainbreaker and giving a playful slap to his cheek. Koji's startled eyes widened and darted nervously. "I heard you're a busy man! First time in Mali?" Koji nodded yes. "Good." John swung toward the middle of the roof.

"So what do you think?" Koji called after him. His accent was less noticeable since the last time they spoke.

John stood still, looking up at the billboard, uncomfortably close, before turning toward him at a distance. "I think," he said with a maniacal grin, "that this is the *ugliest* thing I have ever seen in my life!" His laughter burst into the night air. "We definitely have a situation though. What's your feeling?"

"I think," Koji said, two crooked fingers in the air, "that it's beautiful." He walked toward it, reaching up to touch a strip of acetate on a panel. "But still, could be coincidence," He supposed with a wry smile.

"The monkey that typed *Hamlet*."

"Well I'm anxious to get to the bottom of things, this time."

"Let's hope it's not an abyss." John fixed his eyes on a patch of clear sky to the south. "The timing is right, yes?"

"Linear B and the Vinča signal's probable source is 3.2 light years away."

"She started this series around the time it would have been sent?"

"Possibly both signals, in hindsight."

"You had another look at the research?"

Koji nodded to no one, running his hand along the ledge and peering down into a narrow alleyway as they walked the perimeter. "Where's the rest of it?" he asked, "At the institute?"

John turned to face him, perplexed. "...You didn't stop at the gallery on your way up?"

***

The elevator chimed 81, mirrored doors folded in. The sound of a low, ambient hydrocrystalophone reverberated quietly in an unlit, raw concrete entry hall. An enormous welcome desk erupted from the floor in angular brutalism, greenish fluorescent light tubes at its base. A very young woman in makeup and a tailored lycra and gingham dress greeted them in the dark. "Back for more already?" She asked John, smiling.

"Yes, I've brought an art lover with me this time," he winked as Koji clumsily brandished temporary identification.

They walked into one of the large square openings on either side of her, leading to the inside of a lightbox. Every surface, save for the floor and an outer translucent wall, was covered with shimmering work. A forest of square pillars in the vacant space radiated from edge to edge. Seagreen, cyan, and whitewash dominated fluorescent pink and red shards near flat folding black, contrasting with the tone of the exterior paintings.

Koji's mouth hung open slightly as he reached out to touch a wall. "Liquid crystal," he determined, "Antique. Very expensive." The paintings flickered occasionally, cutting to another image from the series. They wandered silently, the dissonant echoing whine of the glass notes growing more invasive.

"These aren't in any particular order, are they?" John's voice echoed.

"No. Timestamped batches were sent to us regularly," Koji replied, the two of them forming dark outlines as they weaved diagonally through the installation. "Painted in approximately the same order. Also similar problem to last time."

"Which is what?"

"Almost half her paintings don't match." Nearly imperceptible pockmark scars near Koji's cheekbones were visible in the harsh light.

"So she gets to the end, then she goes off–piste?"

Koji nodded.

"…Could be a response," John suggested after a beat.

"Or another signal we don't have. Or a piece of Linear B that is still black in the data, so far."

"Any personal theories? Maybe over a *pito*?"

"I need to collect more data… I'm confident an answer is in there," Koji said before rubbing his eyes, "Sorry."

"African time," John grinned in reassurance as they came to the edge of the darkly tinted wall window.

"We have two hours in the morning train, better then."

"Lily's our newest and youngest resident."

A Moorish embrasure in adobe wall framed a flat graphite colored door. John peered through a tiny desert glass peephole, its gemstone cut creating a kaleidoscopic view of the interior. Fragments of a petite female body at all angles danced to the low rumble of rapid music, warping synthetic chords over treble rhythms like leafcutter ants on fragile bark. Multiple skintight monochrome–patterned leggings twisted, holding a series of contorted and vaguely sensual poses. Silk sleeved offcuts punctuated glimpses of pale breasts in the sulfur–filtered light.

"She's suffered from… behaviors of a compulsive nature," Crawford continued carefully, as the three shuffled positions in the narrow mini–foyer next to her quarters. Koji pressed his eye to the multifaceted view next to a silent intercom. The unrelenting music accompanied several inclined views of her hands making an obscenely rude gesture toward the door. He reflexively jolted his head back a few millimeters.

"Did she have a brain abnormality?" John asked as they maneuvered back into the main corridor. Morning daylight streamed in through the glass above branching logwood beams, John's occasional gray hairs glinting in thick brown.

Crawford shook his head. "The residents don't all have the same background," he minimized a slight limp as they made their way around a corner, "Wolfgang's had mental nano–surgery, for example."

He led the men into a door to the left, through a near identical mini–foyer, to an open door on the opposite corner. A row of screw palms bisected their current quarters. Piles of wood scrap surrounded an anthropomorphic wooden shape in a corner, layered heavily with taped or sewn–in bits of various natural and artificial materials. Cascading downward, the materials continued uninterrupted onto the floor.

Behind a large pile of leaves near the back, next to a small exterior window, sat a lanky Scandinavian in black–onyx patterned attire, hunched frozen over a table of textiles.

"Morning Wolfgang!" Crawford called out.

After a long quiet pause, John asked dryly, "...Does he know we're here?"

"He hears and understands everything. Although he doesn't seem to be in a chatty mood."

Wolfgang's fingers silently worked a sliver of metal across the table surface through clashing fabrics, his head at an awkward tilt. He appeared to be in his early twenties.

"He's preparing for the planting ritual," Crawford continued with pride, "All the residents join in."

"Are those gills?" Koji focused beyond the support roots of a palm, indicating to a horizontal collection of narrow slits in the wall.

"They're in the newer areas of the building. I don't find them terribly useful and he finds the sound uncomfortable," the doctor leaned against the door frame. "We take pheromone recordings about once a quarter."

"You might leave them on all the time now," Koji suggested.

Wolfgang's eyes had moved away from his work, saying nothing. His gaze was drawn to waist level. "He seems fixated on your jacket," Crawford noted.

Koji glanced down at the bundle of translucent red and blue tucked under his arm. John, simultaneously bewildered and entertained, offered an open hand in Wolfgang's direction.

"Only if it's not valuable," Crawford warned, looking down his nose as Koji walked cautiously to the work table and held out the rainbreaker.

Wolfgang extended a hand softly without looking at him, said something very quiet, and placed the item on the table. Leaning down to his shoe, he produced a sharp knife and began to violently cut the shiny thin material into long strips.

Koji stepped back in alarm, catching his foot on a root. "They can be a covetous bunch," Crawford smiled as he stood straight, "but he's not dangerous." Koji looked through the skylight for a moment before following John and Crawford out the door.

"He'll disappear into the wilderness for days at a time," Crawford recounted as they walked down the hall, passing an alcove that housed a gnarled citrus tree. "Last month, he came back with a nasty injury in need of medical attention, but otherwise was completely unfazed. He's bizarrely socialized, and has a sort of... conditional toughness, for lack of a better term. Truly extraordinary, I've never seen anything like it."

Crawford paused in front of Kmetra's imposing door, a pinhole blinked white as it slid open. She stood abruptly from a wooden stool in the corner, her burgundy robes swirling as she made eye contact with the strangers.

"Kmetra," Crawford crossed a bar of bright sun to place a hand warmly on her shoulder. "This is Mr. Etna," John introduced himself by his first name as dye-stained fingers reached out to shake his hand, "and Mr. Kurita."

"Pleased to meet you," Koji said, offering the same. "...Do you know why we're here?" Her gaze was unflinching. "Yes? No?" Koji continued, nodding, then shaking his head. Silent and motionless, her eyes began to shift around the room. Her brow furrowed. She looked back to her work table, the glass smeared at the edges with pink, its delicate titanium folding legs covered in a dark sea of dried rainbow grime.

"Mmm hmm," Koji encouraged. Kmetra looked back at him momentarily, her face showing strain. She retook her seat, a blue cotton bandana wrapped around her head in a long fold down to the middle of her back.

Crawford nodded. "You're welcome to stay and watch for a while."

John crouched in the sun, leaning eagerly for a better angle as Koji scanned the room keenly. The sprawling trees in the kitchen area held bursting ripe fruit. Beyond it, a concrete spiral staircase led down a small trap door, emitting a dim blue-green from the subterrain. Aside from a tall heap of fresh supplies and dark splashes of spilled color overlapping in her work area, the room was clean and uncluttered. "May we see her latest work?" Koji asked.

"Of course," Crawford smiled, crossing the room and calling for Dr. Blanca after leaning out the door.

"Stop trying to organize everyone," John suggested quietly to his partner, settling comfortably on the floor with an arm over one knee while footsteps approached in the hallway.

***

"The man can be rough," Maisie cautioned, "Just step outside if he gets too intense."

"I've just been in Wolfgang's quarters," Koji noted.

"Little Gaspar? He's a sweetheart," she pushed the door open slowly, keys jingling against the fossilized wood, "Stay a meter away from the cage please."

A deep red light washed over Koji as he stepped onto the greenhouse, craning his neck upward through the wire mesh. Kmetra's perspelx overlaid the entirety of the inclined roof, filtering the sun like stained glass. Maisie stepped in the dirt behind him, her dark green suit turning black.

A low grumble resonated from a distance. Maisie turned her attention to the wilting overgrowth. In a distant corner, a figure in charcoal attire lay in open dirt near a totemic circle of carved bark.

"What are you doing Milles?" Maisie called out.

"Witchcraft!" He hollered back, propping himself on one arm.

"Color palette is the same," Koji observed quietly, the magenta and fluorescent red and purple chunks dwarfing the cooler temperatures.

Maisie seemed curious. "You recognize anything from the new signal?"

Koji squinted, tilting his head. "Hard to say. Overall, seems more... rectangular," He risked a guess. "Have these been photographed yet?" The low growl came again, sounding like the distant roar of a lion, well beyond the walls of the institute.

"That's my friend out there..." Milles pointed east to the sound outside, before staggering to his feet. "Don't put on a show for the visitors, Maisie."

She sighed lightly. "This is Mr. Kurita, from UNEXA."

"UNEXA!" he ambled closer, "I'm the extraterrestrial you're looking for." A wry smile from the scruffy face of a mid–forties white man. He pointed upward with a dirty right hand in benediction. "I speak that language. I teach it."

Koji stared at him squarely. "What's it say?"

"You motherfuckers," Milles boomed with disdain, "got no map. You're little children, lost lambs. Get me a pole, and I'll *show* you the way to go. Quit holding on so tight!"

"Okay, *enough*." Maisie sounded exasperated.

Koji peeked around his shoulder, unflustered, to the circular group of free standing branch–log sculptures in the distance. "Is that your creation?" he inquired. Each was over a meter high, vertically and crudely chopped in half. A river of savage, abstract symbols were intricately carved in deep relief.

Milles' icy gaze held steady as he swayed back and forth. "*You* tell him!"

Maisie pinched the bridge of her nose and closed her eyes.

"The symbols look similar to data structures from here," Koji observed, narrowing his eyes at the bark.

"Daddy was a programmer," Milles' voice was tense as he stared Maisie down. "Go on!"

"Does this guy shout down everyone around him?" Koji asked the doctor incredulously before turning to Milles, "You talk more than enough for everybody here."

"He writes sexual fantasies for artificial intelligence," Maisie spoke evenly.

"You got no jurisdiction in here!" Milles turned, opening his arms. "Used to lock me up when they had business to do," he looked to Koji and pointed a condemning finger to the gaping concrete recess buried in the thicket, "Now I sleep in the dirt. You can't get to me. You know why? I'm free *here*!" Three fingers slammed into his temple as he hissed, "You're the ones in that motherfucking cage, I see you doing time in there! How's that necktie feel?"

***

"–an infrared star," John responded, "extremely close by, relatively speaking. Been catalogued for about a century... don't you read the news?"

"I guess I just wanted to hear it from the source." Crawford bit his lip, lost in thought. Kmetra contributed the peaceful sound of crystalline gel smearing in the ambient sun.

"I can certainly sympathize with that," John countered politely, tilting his head in her direction, "You don't have any guesses? Leads?"

Crawford paused, lingering in his head. "Language isolates, in any form, are a rare and precious thing. They're quite fragile on the way up; meaning is *subtracted* in translation; symbols become forked and tainted. Outsiders have a tough time with that. But here, we let things grow as they *are*, with very good reason... This," he trailed off, gesturing to John without words, "I'm astonished... and somehow proud of her accomplishment, whatever it may be."

Kmetra abruptly pushed a freshly finished panel off the light table, clattering to the floor. Crawford beamed at her, before chuckling to himself. "Accepting mystery comes with the territory here. Perhaps the board will have more answers for you."

***

"When was the last time you talked to AI?" Maisie briskly walked down the corridor with Koji.

"I've read transcripts," he replied.

"You've never had a conversation?" Maisie halted in disbelief. Dangling rose quartz earrings caught the light in inertial movement.

"Why don't you check to see if I'm authorized?" Koji stood by steep stairs, descending to a low door in the subterrain of an inner wall. "I'll wait."

"Look," Maisie said, "all I will say is, she's very good at stimulating your imagination. It's quite a mind warp if you've never had the experience, so I would be careful when reporting what you heard," her voice was low, "versus what you *think* you heard."

She crouched and pressed her fingers to a panel in the wall, a pyroxenite door sliding open to reveal a tiny rock cut chamber a meter below ground level. It was unlit and damp, with one bench carved into monolithic stone. Koji sat on a cotton tea–colored cushion, facing a nearly black living wall emitting faint photons of darkest gray. The door slid shut, silencing the voice of a perfectly calibrated female personality.

"She would come home school, close the door to her bedroom, a long time." An oversaturated, grainy recording of a middle aged couple in matching blue, sitting on a stark porch in unforgiving sun.

"Yes it was then, early womanhood," the man looked off to one side as they spoke a mix of Sudanese and bits of local English, all of it needing translation in subs. "I broke several lock off the door, when she was away."

"Then she wouldn't open to us. She would eat stew and go back. She did her schooling well. She used to stare into the text, but she knew she could disappear, like that. That way," she pointed out of frame.

A long, ovaled conference room cradled a sunken black desk, dark fresnel vents in broken lines, and a half dozen faces in the dark turned toward the screen at one end.

"She also finish, finished early, right before her disappearing."

"She moved to another village near here, a stilt–house. Once per week I would go, knock," he mimed, "no answer, no sound. Dark house in the daytime, locked always. No visitors ever inside, no brothers, nothing."

The woman dragged her finger under her nose. "One day, the door, it was wide open. We only heard she went upriver. Years, seven or eight years ago. We went to look…"

"I took my boat, asked the people, the elders. Nothing. We never heard a story about the 'hermit of Shendi' until you came to know us, here."

An off screen interviewer was interrupted as the film momentarily froze. "Kmetra was over a thousand kilometers from her home, nearly catatonic and in very poor health," a disembodied, smoky male voice resonated from the screen, "You can see her pre–admission voxel pictography here." Crisp filigree detail of a rotating neural system sans brain tissue tinted the conference room a bright white. Pinkish glyphs flashed over intense bundles of wire.

"You see overgrowth of connective matter, characteristic of post–surgical patients entering rehabilitation," the images highlighted over the call of seagulls in the distant background. "This structure," he continued, most of the mental image fading away, "suggests Kmetra feels that her ideas are coming from outside of her." A microstructure had slowly overtaken the wall in an organic, asymmetrical tangle. "...but it's just a feeling, as far as we can tell."

The image cut away to a feed of an Egyptian gentleman in his seventies. Fresnel vents in the conference room opened partway, revealing the last light of the day. A ring of gravel, dotted with large chunks of ferrous rock, bordered obtusely inclined walls.

Chantal sat nearest the screen, engaging him. "How did she respond to rehabilitation?"

"She wouldn't be a resident if she had taken well to it," he scratched white stubble beneath oil black hair. Blue sky filled the open window behind him, along with the subdued clatter of a street market a few stories below.

"Is she capable of speech?"

A ringing doorbell caused him to look right for a moment, offering a profile of his aquiline nose. Footsteps on stone could be heard off screen as he began to answer. "Aside from what I've shown, her mind is normal, no damage, no dysfunction. Nor does she have any vocal damage that would prevent her from speaking."

"Thank you Omar. Anything else you'd like to tell us?"

"Well, I've studied Kmetra's condition to the end of my expertise," he paused, his green eyes smiling, "Are you asking my opinion?"

Chantal nodded slightly, holding her chin.

"Her thinking seems to have... astronomical clarity," his voice carried over the background jingle of keys and female voices in Turkish. "That's more your field, so if you chose to explore, for example, the possibility of a neural structure inadvertently functioning as an antenna, I'd be interested to hear the results."

"We'll do that," Chantal assured, "and we appreciate your time."

"Certainly. Please get in touch if the board can further assist you," he offered with a smile, reaching for his hat and pushing back his chair to stand. A brief click of static as the screen went black. Chantal swiveled her chair to face the group.

"I say we prevent her from painting," Koji stated flatly from across the desk, "until she communicates in a way we can understand."

"Because you *know* she can talk?" John shook his head in vexation, "You just got a little spooked is all, wandering in dark corners."

"I've read Koji's AI report," a dark gentleman in blue chalk stripes spoke up, skimming the text on the desk with a hand, "when he asked about Kmetra: 'she said quote, *stay away from her because she will eat your children.'*"

The words sank in. The light from the vents glowed orange. Carbon nanotube pyramid RAM blanketed the ceiling, deepening their silence.

"There is a lot of 'cross–talk' between the residents," added a young Siberian woman in a slate dress, her hair in a textured braid. "Their work is mingling in a way that's uncomfortable to me."

"It's reason for concern with the UN security council as well."

"She also said Milles is a superhuman being!" John cocked his head in disbelief at the report. "He humiliates artificial intelligence with his *imagination*. Her comment about Kmetra plays into that perfectly," he tilted his hands upward, "Doesn't it bother anyone else that the fiction of a madman is warping our actions?"

"What actions would those even be?" Chantal asked curiously.

The chalk–striped suit spoke up. "Exploration of Aerospace cannot be impeded by these… inscrutable actualization rituals. Most of the institute's funding comes from the same public sources we draw from. I doubt the they could function without it, and it wouldn't take much to persuade the council to restrict it."

"The institute's license for *utere* must have been very lucrative."

"The doctor put that money in a blind trust," Chantal responded, "No one besides Kmetra or her direct descendents can touch it, until she's no longer a ward of the institute."

"Sounds like a man of integrity." John looked past the desk, staring into the rocks.

Chantal turned to John with an expectant look. "What would you have us do?"

"Same thing we did last time. Shift our focus to Linear B and leave this woman alone."

Chantal winced. "We're obliged to follow every lead we have. I can't afford to sleep on this. Is there anything else we can do with her existing media?"

The Siberian spoke bluntly. "We've done everything except fuck those paintings."

Shuddering, overblown rhythms accompanied the jangle of discordant bells and the harmonic drone of crystal glass. Ominous microsamples of a detuned flute bubbled underneath. The airy, formless recording pounded with energy through the halls of the institute.

The low pyroxenite door hissed noisily. A masqueraded figure leapt out of the damp AI enclosure, its face of flat gray rectangular gauze was surrounded by a dozen rows of shining earth toned fabrics, sewn in ruffles. Small bare feet peeked out of a full body grass skirt extending downward from the oversized head. It bounded over to the residents' tiny marketplace in a twisting limbless dance. Long strips of translucent red and blue descended from the mask into the grass, revealing nude glimpses in lightning fast motion.

It bumped conspicuously into Uncle Sasha, a wooden barrow in front of him, then into another masquerader towering over everyone, its giant head swinging in time with the sound. Hands appeared through the skirt grass, pulling the mask off to reveal a pale, lightly freckled redhead of nineteen, bright blue eyes shifting sideways and a small nose between flushed red cheeks. Lily's face glistened with a hint of sweat, her hair mussed as she inhaled fresh air.

The giant next to her continued its gyration, a cone–shaped monster extending in widening concentric rings, scraps crackling in the billowing ripples. Its head, a faceless recycled plastic weave with two narrow eye slits, supported a second rosewood neck that extended upward a half meter, morphing into silicon antlers slathered with tar. The monster glided through the narrow market stalls, occasionally doing a series of shaking bounces and twisting ninety degrees along a straight path. It brushed against a redwood stand, swirling over myriad edibles on display.

Sasha's head bobbed casually with the music, his body relaxed. He caught sight of the giant's pale human hand emerge between circular layers, pretending not to notice as it grasped an orange and disappeared into the folds.

Kmetra traversed the daylit corridor in quarter time rhythm, taking long strides toward a stairway leading to a wooden mezzanine. Broken chunks of a hollow geode shell concealed her face, earthen squares tied with copper wire in featureless geologic texture. Her robes were wrapped in dark chunks of forest and gray foam, mixed with amethyst from the mask's interior.

The giant danced over to the opposing staircase, precariously climbing the rickety steps as it continued its chaotic ritual. Kmetra surpassed him, rising to the narrow landing.

Maisie rounded the corner at a distance. Her gaze was drawn to Lily's buckling and flexing dance in the market, the grass figure's movements morphing into a bizarre optical illusion. On the landing above, the giant's hand appeared again, subtly presenting a clear cube with deep indigo liquid. Maisie looked up to see Kmetra smuggling it into a ripple in her clothes.

"Hey!" The doctor flew up the stairs in protest, straining the bolts in the wall as she did so. Kmetra flung the cube over the railing, its diamond–hard glass leaving a small indent where it landed below. Maisie's expression betrayed exhaustion as she reached out desperately to comfort her. Kmetra virulently threw her hand away, pushing past the giant as she stormed down the stairs and out of sight. Sasha bitterly lobbed the cube into the corner store room, filled with crates and boxes.

***

The screen door slammed on its hinges into the wall. Several bird species flew in frantic circular arcs around the dome. The music took on an open, dimensional tone in the aviary.

Kmetra zigzagged angrily through grass and shrubbery, scattering vultured guineafowl and a flock of chestnut sparrows. A long bandana hung from her head down to her ankles, darkening as she splashed through the winding stream, ignoring bridges and slipping on mossy rocks with impaired vision. A night heron barely escaped her path as she clambered up the opposite bank.

She looked around for a moment, bandana dripping, then placed her foot in the crotch of an acacia and pulled herself up. She climbed further, scanning the ground occasionally as she went.

Around five meters up, she hoisted herself into a hammerkop nest, its giant collection of twigs adorned with a few brightly colored scraps. A panicked hammerkop flew into the glass dome and fell to the ground, stunned. Kmetra removed her stone mask slowly, staring in its direction for a long minute.

A blue eyed jungle crow landed on a high branch in the fork where she sat, breaking her trance. She looked down to see a batch of pristine eggs in the nest, freshly laid. She placed her mask over them directly and gently, held her knees, and rocked back and forth in the clamor of music, birdsong, and commotion in neighboring quarters.

***

Adjetey wiped his brow awkwardly with the shoulder of a shirt sleeve, leaning over the greenhouse roof and prying off another panel of perspelx in tattered work gloves. A dirt clod thumped against the fresh inner pane, momentarily exposing the turnip white of plant roots as it burst against the glass.

Milles stood naked on the ground below, gesticulating wildly. The room wasn't soundproof enough to silence his tirade. His face was beet red as he shouted, digging manically for more plants to pull and rocks to throw.

Adjetey tossed the painting over the concrete wall. The air carried it sideways to a patch of grass below, near several others baking in the sun. He pulled at another, over the cracking sound of a rock, indecipherable ranting, and a flash of freshly uprooted vegetation.

***

Crawford laughed quietly. "I'm eighty three years old," he wedged a book loosely into an open topped crate as he emptied a shelf, "Xaya and I are going to a summer cottage. That's all I know to tell you."

Maisie sat behind his desk in the only chair not stacked with books. Both of them looked drained. A shaft of dusty light in the alcove drew her attention to its round vent, only visible now that a giant bonsai had been dragged to the center of the room. "I wish you'd have a second thought about your decision."

The whistle of the breeze in the vent died down. "Should have trusted my instincts," he shook his head, his voice cracking as he puzzle–pieced a volume into a full crate.

***

Direct sunlight streamed into the greenhouse as Adjetey struggled with the last remaining panels near the wall. Milles' branch sculptures formed a horseshoe at the edge of the baobab trees within, framing scarecrow stilts holding a man sized effigy. Hundreds of short, dried bamboo shoots formed its body, which appeared to be held together with black animal hair.

Adjetey dropped the last panel onto the pile, flattening the grass firmly. He heard Saxo's name mixed in with the shouts below, and avoided looking into the greenhouse as he straddled the ladder. Milles had exhausted his earthly supply of projectiles, but it didn't stop him from hurling concrete–amplified vulgarities toward the institute at the top of his lungs. He ran back and forth menacingly across freshly carved symbols that, from overhead, formed an enormous crude abstraction in the dirt.

[*4 months later*]

Maisie weighed a wax tissue down amidst short grass in a light breeze. Producing a wrapped graphite stick from her handbag, she exposed it and carefully began to drag it across the surface, holding the paper firm. A series of dates appeared, immediately next to braille and small dense text and glyphs, translated and repeated in over a dozen dead languages, tightly filling its rectangular dimensions as she recorded the bas–relief of the hard black basalt underneath.

"Thank you, Crawford," she said aloud to the stone, smiling politely as she rolled the tissue carefully before slipping it into a tube. Puffy cumulus clouds dotted the sky overhead. From within a concealed hole in the ground, a diverse cluster of irises burst open in bloom, breaking the flat landscape.

"I have enough one–sided conversations in my life already," she continued, reaching into her handbag again, "But I've written you a note." She fished out a page, pausing for a moment as she unfolded it, adding fresh charcoal fingerprints.

"I want to start by saying positive things," she cleared her throat, "You'll be happily surprised to hear that *utere fexix* honored their contract to the end. They've always done right by Kmetra, and all of us. Eric's been very kind.

"Gaspar's preparing for harvest season, and he seems more passionate and autonomous than ever, despite the changes. The light is also much better in the greenhouse. So, it's not all bad," She took a deep breath before continuing.

"It feels so very different, though, for so many reasons. My optimism has kept me afloat, but Kmetra's sliding into a place I just can't bear to watch... I want you to know it's not your fault. There's nothing you could have done differently, to avoid this–"

Another pause. A swollen sound surfaced in her voice as she struggled through an apology. She folded the letter, whispering quietly, and placed it in the floral opening. She turned away to wipe her cheek, forming a long gray streak under her eye as the wildflowers swayed in the wind.

Kmetra's studio was empty, but a rustle was audible from the subterrain. Maisie called for her as she slowly crept through the open trapdoor, down the spiral of stairs into glowing dark seagreen.

Freshwater kelp and long stolons of utricularia swayed behind the glass walls of the bathroom. Fresnel vents flooded daylight into the narrow slices of murky water.

Kmetra sat on the floor, intently focused on arranging an assortment of dry leaves in a clear bathtub. Otjize dreadlocks draped over her shoulders, her red robes covered in ashen dust. Her skin looked dirty. She failed to acknowledge her companion, slowly brushing the desiccated foliage in an aimless haze.

Maisie kneeled beside her. "Adjetey is going to stay here and watch things for a while– That means I'm going to go. If you want me to come back, just say anything at all... to *anyone*. Okay?"

She waited futilely for a response. The soft hum of water pumps and dull thudding of music from Lily's quarters was all that disturbed the room, melodic drillings occasionally changing their timbre.

Maisie wrapped her arms around her for a brief moment in a gentle, lingering embrace. Watery reflections bounced on all surfaces. Kmetra stared into the infinite space beyond the tub, her hand movements glacial as the leaves blurred.

***

"You'll get in touch as soon as *anything*, right? You'll keep an eye out for her?" Maisie looked into his eyes.

Adjetey nodded warmly, filling the door frame. A cage of keys hung on the wall in the windowless room behind him. An inclined drawing board flickered various data from the institute. "She's just waiting for you to leave," he winked, his voice tracing Hispanic roots, "I bet you'll hear from me tomorrow afternoon."

They gave each other a tight squeeze, her head in his chest.

"Take care of yourself."

She offered the same, letting her arms drop as she turned down the corridor to the main entrance. Shoesteps on concrete momentarily stopped. She paused on the threshold, fingers tracing the edge of her freshly made graphite recording hanging inside, then closed the ebony door behind her with a final click.

***

Milles was invisible, but panting and low grunts could occasionally be heard. A shaded, deep opening in the ground lay within the darkest area of the greenhouse. A plume of fresh soil flew out, landing softly on leaves and moss.

Kmetra lay motionless on her back in the red–orange dirt and late afternoon sun. Her pupils followed flies as they buzzed around her. The morning backdrop of clouds had disappeared, revealing a giant cumulonimbus upwind in the far distance.

A clamor from the recycling skip caused her to glance right. Wolfgang walked noisily on the debris, the overlong burlap sleeves of his purple–dyed tunic snagging exposed corners as he foraged. Shredded hawk and owl pellets dangled from his trousers, rodent fur and bone woven into a crude tapestry of optical fiber and long dead tree switches.

She closed her eyes, her vision red beneath her lids as she looked toward the sun. The clamoring halted, then was replaced by an increasingly loud, liquid warble. She opened her eyes to a pair of kāmaʻo racing overhead.

"Do you want to make some friends?" A high voice came from the skip. Wolfgang jumped over the ledge, making a crunching sound as he landed near a small pile of his recycled selects. His shoes kicked up dirt as he walked over to her. "The skip is full," he said, "they're going to come and pick it up. Do you want to go with me?"

She blinked up at him, her hand over her eyes.

"No one said you can't help me with harvest masquerade, right? You wouldn't be alone."

She got distracted, looking around at buzzing insects in the air.

"Unless you'd rather stay and birdwatch." He sat empathetically on the ground a couple feet away, resting his elbows on his knees and waving a fly from his face.

"You know what I like about the scrapyard?" He waited a beat before answering his own question, "Everything's so clear in there. It's all artificial. *Zero* nature. It'll all be gone tomorrow. Imagined, realized, and discarded. It's a dream life," he said wistfully, "Nothing else like it... Don't you want to rescue someone's imagination from oblivion?" Kmetra looked over at him as he spoke, staring into a mouse's skull. He spotted the recycling transport as it appeared on the horizon, a wavy white speck in the distance.

"You'd better hurry and make up your mind," he stood, raising his eyebrows, "It's a short ride, we'd be back before dusk." He walked over to the skip and reached for a paper maché mask with translucent button eyes, covered in hay and paint streaks, hanging from a log beam.

Kmetra sat up, dusting herself off as the transport cruised speedily down the path she was on.

"I'd stand here," Wolfgang pointed next to him with a shy, nervous smile, "and sit down when I do." He slipped the mask over his head and held still. The driverless transport slowed as it entered the grounds. Kmetra hustled to the spot he indicated at the last moment.

A large magnetic prong extended outward as the truck crawled forward. Just as the skip was lifted off the ground, they sat simultaneously on the protruding bumper, shuffling into a small recess on their knees. The container noisily emptied and dropped back in place. They gripped ridges on the truck sides as it accelerated in reverse to treacherously high speed. Her dreadlocks flailed as she glanced over at him. The hay of his mask quivered and bits of fur flew off rippling cloth.

***

The sky was the same at their destination, but the scenery was very different. A vast sandswept plain with oblique road forks, cheap modern buildings and garages. Kilometers of chain–link fence and corrugated metals split vacant lots and cottage industries.

They jumped off the slow moving transport and walked forty meters to an open concrete overhang buttressed by round pillars and fluorescent light. Chicken wire glass separated a booth from the dirt floored space and a sizable heap of fast moving recyclables in the corner. Kmetra seemed momentarily frightened by the cackling laughter of a hyena. Wolfgang's expression was unreadable behind the mask as he walked by the booth with a mutual wave to the supervisor.

They passed through a truck sized trefoil arch in the back wall. Rounded pyramids of loosely divided scrap towered over them. Wolfgang pulled his mask off, revealing innocent excitement.

Kmetra followed him uphill, their feet sinking into the sliding mass of broken media, bundles of synthetic textile, bits of plastic wire, acoustic foam tiles. The peak offered a bird's eye view of the long open space, ringed with tall fences under yellowing sky and an arcus cloud looming on the horizon.

They made loose circles through the hills. Wolfgang shared finds with her before they disappeared into a huge anti–static bag. Kmetra was slow and deliberate, occasionally placing a colorful chunk of material into a box, then wandering into another territory.

Wolfgang lost himself in the moment, his surroundings indistinguishable as he moved from one shadowy valley to another in dimming light.

***

A bell in the office buzzed. "Kmetra!" Wolfgang called over the mounds, stuffing last bits into an overfilled bag. She wasn't in the immediate vicinity.

Leonard popped around the arch, accompanied by a leashed hyena with dark spots below its ridged back. He pointed to his broken wrist, jangling his keys. Wolfgang ambled over to him. "Have you seen the woman I was with?"

Leonard shook his head. "Not for a little while."

Wolfgang's eyes widened subtly as his head swiveled around. He darted into the yard again, looping in figure eights from front to back. He came around a corner to see her container, full of rainbow scraps, sitting amongst a spread of cellophane wrappers near a hole in the fence. He peeked through it to see more trash and a thicket of trees and shrubs above a carpet of dry leaves.

He ran up the highest and steepest mound, shouting down to Leonard, "Could she be under here somewhere?"

"We would have heard an avalanche," Leonard assured across the yard, "She's probably gone through the fence, or you would have found her by now."

The bell rang again, longer this time. He mumbled under his breath, desperately scanning the environment. He called her name once more, before carefully placing his mask atop the summit, facing the farthest corners. He hopped and slid down the mass of detritus to the arch, looking back nervously as Leonard padlocked the gate. "You missed the transport," he noted, gesturing in the direction of the road with an aerogel cast. The deep red of sundown had been consumed by cloud cover, rolling south over the plain. Large droplets of rain started to fall in the dust.

"I've made a mistake. I'm going to get help. Not in town."

"Your friend had better be careful out here," Leonard tightened his grip on the leash, "hyenas come around after dark, and if they smell something, they're not so friendly as this fella." Black eyes stared into Wolfgang above a vicious muzzle.

Wolfgang nodded, looking back over the gate one last time. His arms stayed low as he began to jog toward the gray mass like a bushman, in the direction they had come. He crossed the road near a large billboard sitting squarely on a steel post. Its flickering tubes lit transparent plastic, advertising nothing.

Adjetey reclined with his hands folded behind his head, listening to the wayward strum of a nylon–stringed acoustic. Rain hammered the roof mercilessly. The sole window in the control office was boarded up, leaking water in slow drips through a fissure in the plywood.

The room's incandescence suddenly faded to deep amber, fluttering erratically before settling into a slow wavering pulse. The tiny wireless stereo continued to broadcast low fidelity guitar. Adjetey sat up to check flashing white graphics on the drawing board, then, sliding over to the cage on the wall, he stood to remove a large ring of keys.

Music reverberated into the hallway as he walked around a corner, down the long corridor to Kmetra's room. Her door was closed, the pinhole light blinking red every few seconds. He rounded another corner to Wolfgang's, his open door revealing a dark and empty chamber. After ducking into the souterrain, he walked back up the spiraled stairs and made his way to the main entrance.

Outside, the pouring rain soaked into his clothes as he called for Wolfgang over the trees with cupped hands. He narrowed his eyes in the darkness, seeing nothing.

Leaving the front door wide open, he entered the atrium

toward the narrow foyer in front of Lily's room. Placing a hand on the door, he turned a black square up to maximum with a static pop. "Lily?"

A quiet "yeah" was uttered eventually, her voice strained. No music was playing.

"We're having a brownout. Everything alright?"

"...mm hmm."

He left the crackling intercom as he walked out into the corridor. The light dimmed further, flickering like firelight. He glimpsed a shallow puddle reflecting beneath the threshold of the greenhouse's outer door. He proceeded slowly, keeping his keys quiet as he slid the petrified door partway and stepped onto the soil with a squish.

Birdsong was wholly absent. Rainwater flooded in sheets down glass roof panes in blinding polyrhythm, blurring the featureless sky. He peered keenly and cautiously through the diamond–mesh into the dense foliage, the perimeter scarcely lit by faint emergency lighting.

His eyes adjusted, revealing fast moving streams of water flowing in paths of least resistance, flooding the entirety of the open ground space. Its source was unseen, but the torrent moved faster and higher in the interior.

In the far open corner, obscured by branch sculptures, he made out a masquerade head above the outline of Milles' dark coveralls, lying prone in the saturated mud. A sheet of distant lightning highlighted a bloody smear on the back wall.

Adjetey rushed to the cage, turning his keys and swinging the heavy inner door open on its hinges in one swift motion. A loud cracking sound, followed by rolling thunder as Adjetey crumpled, semi-conscious. Milles hovered overhead, perched painfully on the roof of the cage in bamboo masquerade. In his tight grip was a long wooden stick carved to a spear point.

The lights surged and faded as Milles jumped down, bamboo shoots clacking by the hundred, blood spilling from Adjetey's shoulder into the mud.

"You'll have to do, Adjetey!" Milles hollered maniacally as he made wide, menacing circles around him in the shapeless humanoid costume, his blood tipped spear facing inward. His face was a mask of dementia, the bamboo rattling with his rhythmic movements. Adjetey struggled to maintain consciousness, blinking as multitudes of his assailant filled his blurred vision. He reached for his wound in another burst of lightning.

"YOU'LL HAVE TO DO!" Milles sprinted forward and swung a brutal spear crack across his jaw, splitting the flesh open. His body went limp. Milles' savage wailing exceeded the volume of the thunder. Lightning strobed his feral adrenalized sprint through the trees.

***

Floodwater dripped on concrete as two steps fell beyond the petrified wood. Milles' body heaved, exhaling deeply between gritted teeth. "Bad day at work!" He shouted in the halls. He clenched the spear tightly, fresh blood dripping between his fingers.

He stared down the corridor, before mumbling faintly. "…Who's been reading my stories," he said under his breath. He glanced left through the atrium, the open door allowing the storm inside. Maisie's graphite recording flapped in the wind. He tilted his head back slightly, looking upward.

"I SAID, who's been LISTENING TO MY STORIES?!" A deep, growling yell of a question.

"Meeeee!" A squeaky girl's voice answered through a sheet of static.

Milles lowered his gaze and exhaled, his face twisting. The spear dropped to the floor with a clatter, revealing a long gash on his palm as he made his way through the empty, darkening corridor.

***

Frantic inhaled gasps and ragged choking breaths interrupted subvocal moans through the static. Milles stood crookedly in the mini–foyer, his voice low and quiet as he murmured fragments of a filthy and humiliating narrative through the black box in the door.

"I'm going to get the keys," Milles intoned, "and you're going to do *exactly* as I say." He stood listening to Lily's amplified ecstasy as a faint affirmative whisper escaped between a crescendo of moans.

His trance was broken with the deafening *thwack!* of a spear against the wall. His head whipped around to see Wolfgang standing in the tiny room, drenched, holding the weapon at his shoulders in an attack stance. Shards of bone glistened through matted gray fur in the sulfur light.

"WELL!" Milles boomed, glaring, "look who's on an express train to the spirit world!"

Wolfgang said nothing, breathing steadily through his nose as he maintained intense, unwavering eye contact. Adjetey's keys dangled from his belt.

"I *know* you! You got no bravery without that mask, boy!" Milles stared back into his eyes. Lily's gasps quickened, amplified in the tiny chamber.

"A half–monster with a trembling stick," Milles continued, watching the point of the spear start to vibrate, "I see your fear!"

Wolfgang nodded abruptly. "I've never killed a man before tonight." He tightened his grip on the crude weapon, dripping rainwater as he leaned on his back foot.

"That makes *one* of us," Milles stared him down coldly, swaying slightly back and forth in aggressive agitation. Lily sounded like she was close.

Wolfgang narrowed his eyes. "You're finished. You know why?"

"Don't play that game, boy! That's your reflection! You can't enter my circle," he hissed.

Wolfgang jerked his head over his shoulder. "See the gills behind me?" Milles' eyes darted to a row of slits in the floor, as Wolfgang went on evenly, "They're recording. Everyone can *smell* your fear. You'll be remembered as a coward–"

Milles lunged with lightning speed, releasing the deafening roar of an attacking warrior as he overpowered his opponent and sent him to the floor. The spear's tip found a gap in the bamboo, Milles howling as it landed, before tearing it away from his ribs and pummeling Wolfgang with tight fists. Lily screamed, her choking breaths reaching a smothered climax in overblown white noise. Wolfgang defended himself from hits and landed his own, despite having the low ground. Milles ran over him, bolting furiously through the doorway and sprinting down the corridor.

Wolfgang kept one eye shut as he coughed and struggled to his knees, feeling a trickle of warm blood in his wet hair. A single whimper crackled into the foyer, followed by a quiet, tearful shudder. He stumbled to Lily's door, looking through desert glass into a black void.

***

The torrential downpour outside the institute was relentless. Lightning flashed, momentarily exposing the deluged grasslands. A series of crashing sounds preceded a loud bang on the boarded window outside the control office. A second bang and the wood flexed, popping a crack down its main fissure. A second later, slivered plywood projectiles flew outward as the drawing board crashed through it, broken semigraphics blinking in the grass before succumbing to the rain. Faint interior light outlined Milles' climb through the splintered portal, trampling over debris and scanning the knoll wildly.

He ran east at full speed, breathing raggedly in near darkness, descending further into the thick gallery forest. *"Where are you!?"* He cried out, spreading his arms wide, palms smacking tree trunks. He rampaged over branches in the dirt, leapt over dead boughs and slalomed through acacias. He repeated his question, longer and louder. A warning roar bellowed from a lion at less than thirty paces. He roared back, charging toward the beast under a series of bright flashes into an explosive collision.

Rain poured into the open storm channel. Kmetra shivered on soaked asphalt under large thin paper sheets, huddling near a metal grate above a steep hole. She squeezed her eyes shut in lightning, her dreadlocks splayed across the asphalt, the otjize melting into the drone of passing runoff.

Moonlight shone through the water in deep walls, a low spectral glide came through waterwheel plants and a forest of kelp. Kmetra stood in her bathroom, water running into the sink as she stared into a mass of flowing black fabrics submerged in jade water. Their rippling disguised a faceless anthropomorphic shape, moving slowly with the current and holding an unseen object. Kmetra focused on it until she found herself submerged, swimming through muck and translucent chambers, tangling her robes as she broke through the surface canopy.

A clear, moonlit meadow surrounded by tall bamboo framed a figure cloaked in anorthosite–mesh. It held a luminous rainbowed mass, the pool mirroring its colors as she emerged. The figure disappeared into silent leaves. Kmetra gave chase, watching reflections of colored liquid in the thicket ahead of her as the figure weaved into denser foliage.

She gained ground, parting the grass in a hollow to reveal the object shining in the soil beneath her feet. Upon grasping it, time and space dilated in her hand. Her movements slowed to near frozen.

The surrounding forest expanded, then billowed inwards, swallowing her.

She was in the foothills of a small mountain, trudging up a winding path past a torch–lit village of straw and mud huts. She scaled the mountain in the dark, the wide spectrum of light guiding her way as she passed the treeline, reaching a dizzying height as the inclined path narrowed to a precipice.

Nearing the summit, she paused to view the urban glow of polluted dawn rising from the ground far below, the horizon a fuzzy greenish–gray. A deep, loud booming sound disturbed her reverie. She looked down to empty hands, the landscape blurring as she turned around. Milles' filthy clothes caught the emissions of the spectrum, his muscles taut with the effort of a focused sprint. Boom. Kmetra bolted after him, her feet crunching pebbles and grinding dust as Milles disappeared into a cave hole.

Kmetra ducked in, moving quickly toward the oil–slick reflections on jagged rock. Milles leapt behind boulders and scurried into deeper crevices that Kmetra had no light to shine in. Water dripped and the walls turned to crystalline structures as she lost ground. Boom. Her expression contorted painfully, watching a rainbow refraction glint through quartz, the sounds of his sliding footsteps becoming more reverberated.

The quartz and tanzanite twisted, defying gravity and any sense of direction. Time dilated further, the crystals darkening into magnetite as ferrofluid slowly entombed her in claustrophobic pitch. She watched helplessly as her treasure descended into the earth, fading into abstract shards of glimmering color.

[3 years later]

Kmetra lay in near perfect darkness. *Boom.* Her eyes opened slowly and slightly. She rolled over to see the faint outline of a black wooden dome woven overhead. Her pupils contracted as she peered to the side through a single round opening.

A natural split in rock, several meters high, let the only light in. The smell of sea mist and the first subtle twilight purple of dawn beneath overcast sky. The sound of waves crashed in the distance.

Dusting her robes and rubbing sleep from her face, she crawled clumsily over the indistinguishable figure laying beside her, hands leaving the damp ground as soon as she had room to stand.

***

The grays of high–altitude cloud cover and ocean absorbed the shifting colors before sunrise, two massive surfaces reflecting off each other. The belt of Venus faded above the horizon as Kmetra peered into it, surrounded on the cliff's edge by billowing susuki grass.

Boom. Nearly a kilometer behind her, well beyond a long sculptural fence of iron gauze, a monstrous industrial crane emblazoned with glowing blue–white katakana hammered pillars deep into the ground.

Her gaze shifted downward. The receding tide filled and emptied a wide, shallow pool. Further out, bioluminescent algae emitted a soft, submerged glow. The light remained stationary as the ocean moved over and through it, occasionally permitting the bright edges of an artificial structure to break the surface.

***

Her bare feet left dry prints in mud as she walked sixty meters into the sprawling tidal basin. She untangled a mound of hemp netting and kelp to uncover a cache of glowing jars secured to the rocks, tied in pairs. She tugged at a rope and ducked under it, then placed a second one behind her neck. The jars swayed freely near a bump in her abdomen.

She continued further out, into a labyrinth of ataxite–colored metal slabs several centimeters thick and two meters high, indifferent to the undulating ebb and flow of waves passing through them. She rounded corners, walking through narrow channels, approaching an assemblage of vertical fluorescence. She stepped over a bundle of tiny cameras moored to the structure and into ankle deep surf.

Dipping a synthetic brush in a clear jar of liquid, she wiped broad strokes across the substrate, before opening a radiant hot pink and spreading a deliberately slow and thin emulsion across damp gray. Farther down the corridor, leprose lichen emitted increasingly vivid colors, powdery arcs of brilliant blue and mauve cut across a jumble of deep green polyform segments and flecks of dark metal shavings. Asymmetrical repetition of form down the halls dissolved into a demolished film strip, thousands of red and yellow particles bathing in seawater.

As the tide rose, she navigated to higher ground, making her way to the outer walls. She glanced backward over a foaming prominence of rock, catching a glimpse of orange firelight in the cliff opening.

***

The gate creaked loud enough for them to hear. It slammed shut, Wolfgang's eyes instinctively moving upward from a steaming titanium cup. Dressed in dark hemp and seaweed, he scratched at messy hair as he looked across the embers. Kmetra sat hunched, smiling at him as she scooped blackened fish into her mouth.

The sound of labored breathing accompanied Alma's appearance at the entrance, lifting herself by the poles of driftwood jutting from volcanic cliff rock. Wolfgang jumped up to help her, lending a hand as she steadied herself on the damp floor. "You alright?" He inquired.

"Oh my yes," she assured him, giving a warm pat to his arm, "just getting older." They walked to the embers, where she sat seiza–style with a light groan, her crisp suit protected by a blanket in the dirt. Wolfgang poured coffee from a black kettle and placed the cup in front of her as she unzipped her bag.

"We have enough breakfast, if you'd like some?" Wolfgang offered, the skillet sputtering with warm food.

"That'd be nice, thank you," she smiled broadly, deepening crow's feet as she produced a jar of lambent indigo from her belongings. "New species, just for you. Arrived from Sfax yesterday." She pulled another in cadmium yellow. Kmetra stared at them as she gently placed open palms on Alma's cheeks.

"We're obviously both pleased to see you," Wolfgang presented a sizzling plate in front of her, "What brings you to all the way to Kagoshima prefecture?"

"That's a fair question," Alma blew on a chunk of panga and then munched with delight, "I'm a little surprised to be here myself."

Wolfgang looked over at Kmetra, who was oblivious as she grabbed a jar for inspection. Cinders crackled. He returned focus to their guest.

"I received word that a UN hearing is scheduled for this afternoon," Alma continued after a sip of coffee, "They've indeed asked for Kmetra to be there."

Kmetra absent–mindedly traced shapes on the glass with her fingers as the musical call of an Aleutian tern soared beyond the rocks.

"The board would like her to go," Alma nodded, ducking her head near Kmetra's line of sight, "But the decision is yours to make."

Wolfgang looked on as her dark brown eyes stared hard into the lichen, reflecting their colors. Kmetra leaned back to stand, swinging long half–up box braids behind her. Through the rock split, morning cloud cover framed their silhouette as she circled the fire to embrace him, one wrist on his neck as she cradled the back of his head.

Low murmurings of several hundred people filled the atrium as they returned from recess. Nearby voices became quieter as Alma, Kmetra, and Maisie formed a single line to pass through a crowded entryway.

The hemicycle was vast, lit by curved fresnel walls and a ceiling that matched their color temperature. Classical columns supported marble statues, sharp and multifaceted abstractions of dynamic movement frozen above the speaker's floor.

Kmetra traversed the aisle, her sandy moccasins shuffling beneath black robes. Escorted to their seats, Maisie surveyed the room as they waited for the undertone to die down. She caught sight of John in the mezzanine and waved discreetly to him. He returned her greeting, then raised an eyebrow in question as he mimed a pregnant belly with his hands. Maisie glanced at Kmetra before nodding to him, momentarily covering her face with her hand in a mask–like gesture.

A gentle tapping sound from an undetectable location silenced the room within a few seconds, as a light skinned man in a dense knit gunmetal suit approached the floor, folded pages in hand.

"Welcome back, ladies and gentlemen. I will now moderate a brief, informal hearing on an addendum to the golden message." He paused for a beat. "Next week, in an unprecedented event for humanity, a message aimed specifically at extraterrestrial life will be broadcast in infrared from the lunar base at Malapert crater. This message has been historically curated by the Golden Message Subcommittee, who we thank for their challenging efforts over the years, working with the public to select exemplary cultural and scientific achievements to send to the stars.

"The signals we've received over the last six years have inspired us to rethink our place in the universe. Alas, any conclusive understanding of the data have remained elusive.

"This young woman," he gestured in a gentle sweep to Kmetra as heads turned, "has been creating media that not only preceded, but is visually almost identical to the exosolar transmissions. She's also created voluminous additional work that appears to be in the same format, in all three cases well before the signals were received."

Kmetra stared upward, ignoring the gazes of others as she examined the organized chaos of tangled microphone twigs hanging far overhead. Various members covered one ear to concentrate on earpieces.

"As you may know, Kmetra has not communicated to anyone verbally for her entire adult life. Numerous attempts to interpret this phenomenon from a scientific standpoint have proven unsuccessful. The tone and content of her 'responses,' if you will, are a mystery. While truly remarkable, there is significant reluctance within the UN about sending her work to a likely intelligent recipient.

"The full report of her history is on file. I encourage you to read it carefully before submitting your vote. Our seats in Mexico City will also hold a hearing on this issue in a few hours. By late tonight, all member votes will be cast."

He looked out over the curved benches. "With us today is the director of UNEXA, Chantal Guerrera." Chantal offered a stoic acknowledgment from the back of the room, holding her chin.

"Dr. Maisie Blanca, a researcher at the institute where Kmetra resided for several years," Maisie raised a hand in the air briefly, "And a board member from the institute, who are collectively here to answer any questions you may have. Thank you all for coming."

He cleared his throat as he held the pages above his head. "Before we begin, I have a pair of pre–submitted statements," he flipped them open with a rustle, "The first is from Fayrouz Xenakis, representative for the Egeria Martian Colony. She asserts that an honest and important facet of this message is a concession to the unknown.

The colony is solidly, unifiedly behind Kmetra's work. They intend to vote in the addendum's favor. Her full remarks are available for review.

"I also have a brief statement from AI," he continued, "which I've been requested to file, though unfortunately its abstruse musings don't appear to indicate a clear or actionable point of view."

He paused again, folding the pages into a breast pocket. "Before we open the floor, I would be remiss not to ask Kmetra if there is anything she would like to communicate to the UN body. Kmetra?"

The members turned in unison toward her. Kmetra's fingers twitched in her lap as she stared ahead to the speaker with professional poise and an unreadable expression. Maisie exhaled audibly through her nose. A long silence passed, disturbed only by a cough and the tinny trail of delayed translations from earbuds.

The moderator gave an understanding nod and the trace of a polite smile. "Very well. Our first speaker is Rebecca Deodato, representative from Iceland."

A brunette in a steel blue suit and palmwood hair clasp strode down stepped semicircles to the floor, flashing a smile to the moderator. She appeared to be in her mid fifties, wearing a silvery pearl blouse and a brooch of bismuth crystal.

"Kmetra's recent works are the most watched non–narrative media on the planet. I love them, and their popularity is unquestionable." She looked around the room with the composure of a seasoned orator. "But we're in a moment of enormous magnitude. This message may serve as an ambassador to another civilization. We can't afford to communicate a dangerous ambiguity or a possibly threatening tone.

"Kmetra has an understanding of language and the ability to speak. To imply that she's selective or taciturn, would be a mammoth understatement. Her stubborn refusal to communicate with anyone around her, the lethal instability of concurrent residents at the institute, and her history of illness are all cause for grave concern."

She turned to Alma and Maisie sympathetically. "Please forgive me for speaking so frankly. It's not a criticism of your work, for which I have tremendous respect. I only object to the context," she assured them before turning back to the audience, "The Golden Message represents a razor–thin slice of our output as human beings. I recommend we support the hard work that went into compiling it, and exclude the media in question–"

The opening glissando of a Mexican harpist bloomed across a small bare stage, his only accompaniment a vibrant Otomi rug beneath him. An intimate audience slowly burst into rowdy, enthusiastic applause in recognition of the piece, whistling and shouting.

In a grand adjacent chamber by the back window, Chantal picked up the last bit of miniature corn flautas from a small plate, checking her bracelet as it flashed updates. John looked over, stifling a yawn.

"If she would just vibrate some air over her vocal cords," Chantal lamented rationally, "This is beyond aggravating." She tilted her bracelet toward him, nervously tracing the basket weave of hair behind her head. Her tone was anxious. "They're voting now. You're not really going to go through with this, are you?"

John was incredulous. "We have been *hideously* unfair to this woman. If this doesn't happen, I'll be on the first flight home tomorrow," he said with resolve as he reached for a half–empty glass, "Anyway, I can't roughhouse with my kids on a call."

Kmetra appeared in the opposite corner, taking broad strides through tables, her trailing fabrics snagging on a passing waiter as she made a beeline in the wrong direction. Maisie burst in a few seconds behind her, walking briskly with clenched fists as she corrected her course and led the way to their table.

Greetings flowed among them. John offered a hand to Kmetra, which she briefly held like a child, looking at Chantal. She nodded silently to Kmetra with a smile.

"A drink maybe?" John offered as Maisie took a seat.

"And some food," she agreed, "I'm sorry we're so late."

A young Japanese woman arrived from the bar with an open bottle while Maisie fumbled with a card on the table. Chantal ordered in fluent Spanish.

"Perhaps I should order for Kmetra," John suggested.

Maisie laid the card face down, hiding its kanji. "For us both, please."

Kmetra remained standing, gazing out the window from inside her hood. The tiniest sliver of dark sky was visible through its smoky tint, stars crashing into architecture. The northwestern view was smothered by the sixtieth floor of an adjacent mixed–use building. As the server passed beside her, Kmetra held a steady hand over the top of her wine glass.

John addressed their waitress in thick, broken Japanese as she suppressed a giggle. Chantal leaned over to Maisie, grinning behind her hand. "Koji loved when John spoke like this. Never failed to make him laugh."

"Will Koji be joining us?" Maisie asked.

"No, he's resting. Lots of preparation, big day tomorrow."

The waitress left as John wrapped up their stilted conversation. "Good last meal," he hinted, winking slyly at Chantal.

Kmetra darted away from the table, knocking her empty glass onto dark red linen as she zigzagged swiftly back where they had entered. They all craned their necks to follow her path, Chantal rising from her chair.

"Let her go," Maisie sighed, raising a hand slightly from the table, "she's been really restless all evening."

Kmetra passed the concert brusquely, through columns of dark wood and glazed sunburst tile, then a narrow alley of blossoming jacarandas and double doors spilling into a closed indoor hall teeming with pedestrians. She clutched her abdomen, disappearing into the throng.

***

"–Milles is buried in the greenhouse," Maisie finished her story over clay cazuelas, her companions in rapt attention, "And there's a lion out there, with the most *unusual* scars I have ever seen in my life." She gazed wide–eyed into space, before forking a bite from her plate.

Chantal and John exchanged a look. "Is Lily still a resident?"

"Mmm," Maisie swallowed a mouthful, "She's doing so great. Really unbelievable turnaround, a very sweet young woman. Her work is... unreal." She beamed with pride.

Chantal's bracelet illuminated softly. She scrunched her face while reading, then turned her wrist awkwardly to John. He shook his head, furrowed and scornful. Maisie followed the interaction between the two with a puzzled expression.

"John promised to resign if Kmetra's work isn't allowed to be broadcast," Chantal offered an explanation, "And unless I can change his mind... we will miss him dearly."

Maisie's mouth hung open in shock. She seemed tense, almost tearful. A long frozen moment passed.

"You okay?" Chantal seemed genuinely concerned for her.

"...I was so sure they would do it," she managed, breaking from her trance, "I just, don't know how to tell her..."

"I'll do it," John slid a chair back angrily as he stood, "I need a walk anyway. Where would you go, if you were her?"

***

The crowd was much thinner at the end of the enclosed pedestrian street. The forest of concrete tapered to a sloped corner, a tiny black door offsetting walls of pale gray. About ten meters away, a pair of buskers filled the vicinity with the playful sounds of a cello stick and nano–melodica. A small gathering of colorfully dressed young women clapped along, collectively forming a galloping rhythm.

From a distance, John appeared to mime to the bouncer outside the door. Hands overhead for the hood, long flowing robes as his hands descended to his knees. The bouncer nodded, saying something as he gestured toward the door, then shrugged his shoulders.

John walked over to the young group. Two of the girls doubled over in laughter as he began to talk, disrupting the rhythm they'd created. He continued undeterred as they strained to listen, wincing with broad smiles, until one attentively put a hand on his forearm. She nodded in affirmation as they walked together to the door.

***

Needle thin white optics lit the length of a narrow passage in an otherwise throbbing rush of darkness. Rounding a corner to an inner opening, a tiny plaque discreetly introduced the

NEW TOKYO LUGALBANDA

below lucent katakana.

John thanked his temporary partner as they crossed the threshold into loud, atomically sliced glitches of harmony. She winked at him in parting and sidled up to a glowing bar in the lobby. He squeezed through a dark archway, the other side shimmering with sparse spectral bokeh. Warping columns with polygonal mirrors at odd angles created impossible barbershop infinities, blending the high polish of reflective floor, walls and low ceiling into one disorienting whirl.

He walked forward carefully, glimpsing fragments of dancing feet, half a man's face exhaling a vapor, the swirl of translucent multiprisms, his own hand stretched into a flesh colored line that curved upward and distantly collided with a dim magnification of an airless ice cube on the bar behind him. Once he was a few steps inside, it was impossible to tell the dimensions of the room, or if multiple spaces might be connected by the precision bouncing of photons across surfaces and bent through angled glass.

One foot moved in front of the other. He scanned with his head tilted, blinking slowly. The meter of the music's rhythm seemingly folded in on itself every few seconds. He nearly bumped into a pair of dancing couples who remained invisible until he was right in front of them. Looking over a lady's shoulder, he caught a triangular section of black robes slowly drifting in purplish light. He moved toward it, watching the reflection ripple up into the ceiling before disappearing. He paced backwards until he found it again, then turned in all directions.

Squarely behind him, Kmetra sat in a black pyramidal nook, cradling something in her arms. John approached her through the kaleidoscope of silvery color and punishing bass. She seemed unaware of his presence. A small white wicker doll sat nestled in her sleeves, arms and legs and torso woven together meticulously with hand dyed twigs. A glass jar formed the head, the wood twisting into a helmet–like covering over the top, leaving its face exposed. A stepped, clear acrylic shape inside flickered with ambient light.

The launch terrace was peacefully nestled in a low hillside under cloudless midday sky. Slate flats in the near distance cut a stadium sized rectangle into nature. A voice announced seventy seconds to launch, yet no ship was visible.

"Kmetra didn't want to watch?" Chantal blocked the sun with her eyes atop a low square turret adjacent to the bleachers. Children scrambled to distribute temporary binoculars below, as they swung on flaking gray–green railings over the protests of their parents.

"She's still on the facilities tour I guess," Maisie waved a hand dismissively, clinging to the binoculars in her lap. "Enthusiastic colleagues you have here, some big admirers."

"You seem a bit disappointed," Chantal observed. A docking bay opened in the ground hundreds of meters out, revealing a deep octagonal silo with long soot markings scraping inner walls.

Maisie took a deep breath, regaining her composure. "I think I'm just tired from yesterday. Now that my testimony is done I'm eager to get back to work."

"I know the feeling." Chantal's tone was empathetic.

"They need me there. And Kmetra's just impossible. I'm grateful the board took on that responsibility. Not that they seem too involved these days..." Maisie paused. "Did John, uh–"

"Unfortunately he's on a flight home to Athens." The countdown entered the low twenties as low rumbles and hissing whine of air compression echoed from the vertical cavity below. "Man of his word."

Fifteen seconds. "I'm very proud of Koji," she pivoted, holding binoculars toward the cement gap as the lenses darkened, "He's a brilliant scientist, with very good instincts. He'll make a great addition to our team up there. We feel very lucky."

The last few seconds filled with the preparatory sounds of combustion, spectating families quieting down as they gazed toward the cacophony of igniting fuel.

At zero, a cluster of snowy trapezoids and polarized glass shot out of the ground, its trail of tuned flame and billowing smoke vibrating the terrace as the ship accelerated past 300 kilometers per hour in the span of a few seconds.

Maisie's binoculars locked and auto–zoomed to its target just as the sound barrier shattered, the winged craft arcing against clear blue as it jittered in magnification. A pillar of clouds were drawn by a spark of red, ever smaller as it angled out of the upper atmosphere.

"Keep an eye on it," Chantal said as she peered into the sky, smiling beneath her optics. "If we're lucky we can see the separation."

***

Koji and the pilot sat braced in chairs that absorbed the brunt of g–forces they were experiencing. "Stand by for fairing and booster separation," the pilot announced calmly, gripping an armrest in the shuddering hull, receiving notifications from an earpiece and the display of the flight deck. The cone of oblong windows frosted as thin gasses whooshed over them in diminishing amounts. "Go for separation."

The hollow, metallic twonk of pyrotechnic bolts shook the craft momentarily, a brief flash of white above the windows as clamshell fairings flared open, rapidly spiraling outward as the angular ship hurtled forward in now zen–like silence. The ventilation hissed as the floating sensation of low earth orbit caused them to rise slightly in their chairs.

A series of graphics flashed in bluish–green. Koji checked his pulse, eyeing the disciplined calibrations of the pilot.

"Preparing Hohmann transfer," the pilot announced to the ground as second stage engines whirred to life, rising in pitch.

The sound of tumbling below the floor caught Koji's attention. "I hear loose cargo down in mid–deck," he leaned against his velcro restraints in the direction of the pilot.

"Have a look after the transfer burn is complete?" He reasoned, not deviating from the maneuvers at hand. "Give me twenty minutes."

***

Koji grasped a ladder at the rear of the flight deck, under a pattern of winding organic circuits embedded in panels of dark fiberglass. He angled his legs down through the hole, clumsily catching his weightless foot on a rung before a half–gliding descent into the space below.

Subtle pinhole daylights highlighted key locations as he floated toward an array of metal shipping boxes. He grasped at canvas belts, checking their security. Nothing appeared out of place as the bundle of cubes floated in their restraints.

Hearing a muffled sound behind him, he turned toward the burgundy wall of sleeping capsules. Pushing off from the cargo, he drifted across to slide one of the doors open. His vision warped the room as he lay eyes on Kmetra, hovering fetally above the bed, vomiting into a pillowcase.

Maisie and Chantal moved swiftly through a doorless hallway cloaked in carbonyl iron, ending in a cubic control room. Megateo listened from a frontal wall screen to a powerfully built officer gesturing over his shoulder through a window. Beyond the glass, men in tailored navy and green stared into bright living walls, scrubbing through myriad angles of fast moving surveillance imagery. "She has a few sympathizers at UNEXA who might have been willing."

"Kmetra doesn't need help getting into trouble like this," Teo noted, "She's an expert." Maisie nodded in agreement as she walked in.

Chantal held a hand up curtly, silently greeting Teo before turning to the officer. "My next call is to the prime minister of Japan. With all respect, we're not here to solve the mystery of our massive security lapse," she pointed skyward. The officer released his thumb from a long desk in front of him, laden with overlapping data. The room dimmed as the security glass behind him went black.

"The crew," she continued, "and our mute stowaway will enter the pull of lunar gravity in 27 hours. While Kmetra's proven very unpredictable, we're guessing her actions are related to the Golden Message ceremony. I need to risk–assess her presence if we reroute to another base."

"There's a report of an object on board," the officer spoke, scanning boxed text illuminating in his desk. An index finger called up the bustling flight center in the same glass behind him. Aside from its distorted projection, the view was eerily lifelike.

"Request a visual please," Chantal instructed the officer before turning back to Teo. "There's no way we're letting her anywhere near that broadcast. Shackleton is a research outpost over a hundred kilometers away. Non–emergency transport between bases would be halted."

"Can't they turn back now?" Maisie looked to the officer.

"It's an ultralight spacecraft, maximum efficiency. Just enough fuel for course corrections and lunar landing."

"Emergency abortion at this stage is reserved for catastrophic system failures," Chantal went on, "so unless you know of a risk to the crew we aren't aware of…"

"Only if she can open the airlock." Teo blinked in his dark surroundings. "She likes to wander," he emphasized.

The officer shook his head. "This situation is far more dangerous for her than anyone else."

Maisie and Teo looked at each other for a silent second.

"They can be home in seventy hours by swinging through a lunar orbit, without landing," Chantal suggested, calling up a display over the glass view of the flight center. "That, and other alternatives, would amount to very expensive delays for numerous endeavors."

The window behind them was overtaken by a blurry snapshot of the white doll, its face reflecting the pin lights of mid–deck. Maisie stared with a widening expression. Behind the outline of its neatly entwined driftwood was a small dark porthole and the edge of weightless robes.

The officer read carefully through flickering updates. "She handed this to Koji from a pouch wrapped around her torso."

Chantal's face went askew as she absorbed the latest disclosure from the ship. "…So, she's not pregnant?"

"She's definitely with child," Teo confirmed.

The officer nodded. "The gills in the facility picked up positive readings," he made a few quick hand gestures across his desk, "Maybe she's not as far along as her appearance would indicate."

"Maisie?" Chantal called out, leaning into the attenuated corridor and catching a flash of blonde hair as Maisie blurred around a corner. Chantal threw her hands in the air, bewildered by her sudden departure. "What is going on?" She turned to Teo, pointing at the doll, "This deception is unnerving."

"Mrs. Guerrera," Teo cleared his throat, "I have a suggestion. I cannot predict, nor can I translate Kmetra's actions. However, this image," he pointed a centenarian hand, "gives me a sense. I have an offer to make to you, in exchange for something. If you agree, we can decide how. The details, etcetera."

Chantal looked up at the screen, hesitant. "Right now, I'm thinking of having her sewn into a straight jacket the moment she arrives," she deadpanned, "This had better be good."

Wolfgang traversed the shallow ocean floor, slowly closing distance for a shot. The iridescent shark catfish darted through shadowy rocks, outmaneuvering him as it disappeared behind a shelf. He peered around the formation, his hair rippling, before looking up to the dark blue surface through fluid goggles. He pushed off, kicking fins diagonally toward the underside of a small boat, his nose bubbling. Layered strings of cowry shells intertwined in a messy dangling weave from his waist above neoprene shorts.

He burst through the surface, blowing water away from his face. He placed one hand on the hull of the whitehall and threw a carbon nanotube speargun inside with the other, steadying himself in the swells as he pulled his goggles off and trained his breathing. A sliver of shimmering orange lingered on the horizon, faint glimmers highlighting distant waves.

Atop the bluffs, he saw a transport moving at top speed behind the sculptural gauze fence. He followed its trajectory, stopping abruptly near the gate. An indistinct figure in bright white ran across the gravel.

***

Maisie descended the cliff by way of a steep and narrow path, then by jutting poles of driftwood, leading down the crag to the rocky beach. "Gaspar!" A gray pelican flew inland overhead as she reached the shore, Kmetra's warren of metal and lichen standing firm in ebb tide. A shallow surge of froth surrounded her feet, rinsing pebbles and sand.

She called out again across the water, the miniature vessel bobbing a hundred meters out. She watched as Wolfgang reached for something inside, then disappeared below the keel. She looked to and fro in anguish for a moment, cursing under her breath as she took off her shoes. Hurling them backward into the sand, she ran into the waves, wading waist high before diving over a crest and swimming freestyle.

She swam against the breakers, losing her breath before she was halfway there. She kept her eye on white wood, drifting unmoored in the current. Her clothes dragged at her as she went underwater against her will. A strained, final push of determination and she grasped the edge of the rowboat, just as a giant fish burst over the other side, flopping violently on its floor while she threw an arm aboard to steady herself. The fish lay gasping, a spear piercing its gill.

A pair of hands opposite hers appeared on the hull. Wolfgang pulled himself up in alarm, then in sudden recognition.

"*Maisie?*"

***

"I made the doll as a ritual," Wolfgang sat across from her as calm water lapped the sides, "for the enormous ambitions we have for our child. Nothing supernatural about it."

"You don't have any idea what it means for her?" She clung to her knees on the back seat. The sun had dipped below sea level.

"I love that woman more than anyone else in the world," he broke eye contact, looking to the beach. "She's still capable of surprising me," His hand reached into the gill of his deceased catch, pulling the spear out neatly. "Whatever she's doing, she doesn't need our help."

"That's your family up there," she implored, "She's risking *everything*."

"Look at this!" Wolfgang lifted the catfish in the air between them in fading sky, "Its ancestors were a freshwater species. Two centuries ago, they only knew rivers. Now," he spread his arms wide, "it swims in open ocean! No pain. No *fear*. We *imagined* this." He held it high, his tone triumphant. "But that," he pointed to the waxing crescent suspended in a gradient above the horizon, "is pure wilderness."

Maisie nodded behind streaks of wet hair as he released the

catfish into the boat, washing his hands overboard before disconnecting a string of shells from his belt and tying it around her wrist with a smile.

"Ready to go?" he asked tenderly, grabbing the oars and dipping them into the water. Earthshine lit the darkness of the moon, set low among early evening stars as the sky sank into astronomical twilight.

The inside of the spacecraft was enveloped in darkness, their only light reflected from the silvery lunar surface. The pilot's eye twitched, listening to his earbud as he made careful finger gestures across unlit instrument panels.

Kmetra's wide eyes peered through oblong trapezoidal windows surrounding the flight deck. Secured by criss–crossed straps in a chair behind him, she cradled her ligneous cargo and studied surface details as the moon's horizon oscillated with the pitch of the ship.

Koji sat abreast of the pilot, nervously focused on updates through an earpiece. He exhaled through his nose, looking beyond the window to an uninhabited range of ridges and peaks, bisected by harsh shadows. Large polygons of patterned land blended into flat valleys, dense grooves of interlocking anorthosite panels absorbing airless sun.

Their descent steepened, thrusters vibrating the hull in short bursts. The stark terrain rushed into view, sharpening details of rock and pits. A clustered geometry of synthetic structures appeared at the fore, perched on the rim of a crater over twenty kilometers wide.

***

The sibilance of the airlock's broken seal accompanied a rush of sweet smelling air from the other side. A researcher in mismatched green khaki stood in front of long diagonal rows of agriculture, sparsely dotted with people. False clouds drifted imperceptibly against the turquoise sky of a giant glass dome overhead, their low relief and contrast lending the surreal tone of Renaissance oil.

The pilot disappeared swiftly into a neighboring corridor as Kmetra took uneasy first steps in lunar gravity. "We weren't expecting you so soon!" one of the researchers smiled at Koji with a subtle wink, shaking his hand.

Koji gestured toward the man standing to their right. "Kmetra, the tailor will assist you so you can be fitted properly for your time here." She looked over, fixing a deep gaze on Koji. "I'll keep it safe," he said, offering to hold the wooden fetish she clung to. She paused with trepidation for a long moment, before slowly extending it in acquiescence.

The tailor beckoned with a subtle tilt of his head, moving toward a brightly lit adjacent room down a corridor next to the airlock. After a few seconds, Kmetra disappeared behind him as the door shut.

"You couldn't get a look at what's inside this thing?" The researcher peered through the figure's glass jar at the rigid acrylic shape within. Koji shook his head.

"We didn't have an analog reader on board."

The two quickly traversed the dome's perimeter on stepped blocks of basalt, loping around a series of crops. At a low platform on the far end of the curved inner wall, Koji tossed the crude astronaut onto a short round loading pad. The analog acrylic's interior brightly blinked red/amber/green. The avian sounds piped into the dome halted and the room darkened as the sky was replaced by imagery. Researchers stopped their tasks, some holding leaves as they looked upward from crops in the wet soil.

The entirety of Kmetra's recorded work hung in the artificial heavens. A patchy scrapbook of Kmetra's early paintings in phosphorescent splendor filled the far end. Then, a vast central swathe of backlit iridescent perspelx. Over the hum of nearby projectors, the sound of ocean waves lapped against the seashore, permeating the air as countless angles of an iron maze glowed with bioluminescence. Several cameras were submerged, catching bits of debris as the current passed over slabs thick with life.

The researcher with Koji suppressed a smile as he held his head back in wonder.

***

The tailor's workshop was a disorganized melange of ridged, rubbery textiles on all surfaces. Spare body pieces in color coded sizes and shapes formed a giant heap in one corner of the room, Kmetra's robes crumpled on the opposite side. Miniature seaming devices sat on the tabletop among specialized tips.

He connected segments along her body in unpredictable lines, her nearly completed suit a shining, quilted abstraction of high visibility colors. A retroreflective chestpiece in deep red was obtusely sutured to a long triangle of pale mint over one shoulder, into a warped kite shape of pink pastel, angling down to deep electric blue over her left forearm and hand. Restless digits flexed in discordant orange and yellow dayglo.

The door opened, revealing Koji alone in the corridor. He looked over to Kmetra, then scanned the tailor's work as he finessed seams with his back to him. "Have time for one more?"

Koji and Kmetra began their descent in the vacuum of the clear funicular, down a railway into an impenetrable shadow. The interior was lit from its edges by exposed blacklight tubes, fluorescing the various fragments of their bespoke suits into blinding complementary colors.

The vehicle accelerated smoothly and swiftly downward. Koji watched the crater's ridge shrink in the distance. Kmetra held the violet–white of her doll tightly in both hands.

He looked into her glass helmet as she stared ahead, her braids tied back beneath a rectangle of opaque plastic, the light reflecting in her irises and highlighting white teeth.

"I feel like I'm hallucinating." Her radio picked up his low voice. The sinewed pastiche of his suit highlighted his slightly muscular frame. The funicular vibrated as it hurtled into the pit.

"I don't understand why this circumstance has been agreed to," he addressed her as they started a gradual deceleration, "but you're held responsible for your actions out here. You understand that, don't you?" He paused for a recognition, receiving none. "You answer for yourself from now on. The board isn't taking care of you anymore," They glided swiftly in deep inky blackness, the incline of the railway gently curving toward the crater's floor.

"...And neither am I," he added with finality.

The silent vibrations stopped as the blacklights dimmed. He aligned his eye toward an ultraviolet biometric square near the door, which then soundlessly opened outward. A huge arc of dark blue lights unshuttered on the ground outside, fluttering to life.

They slowly approached the faintly illuminated underside of a giant lenticular shape, its brim at shoulder level, its width close to three hundred meters. They ambled closer, clouds of dust kicking into the underlight.

Kmetra slowly climbed a narrow metal staircase attached to the edge. The inside of the concave structure was filled with an ionic liquid, its perfectly still surface reflecting an inverted sky. High above, the crater's rim formed a crescent of permanent sun, cradling a multitude of stars.

Koji traced the telescopes' boundary. "Lots of work to do," he lamented audibly, murmuring on the radio under his breath, keenly investigating the equipment. He looked up at Kmetra, barely visible as she kneeled over the water, her helmet pressed against the effigy. A long moment passed before she lowered it solemnly into the liquid, lifting her arms out and letting it drift from the shore.

His eyes traveled back to the surface reflection. He stared in profound amazement as constellations and faint smudges of galaxies began to warp in uncannily high ripples, propagating outward from the bobbing surface disturbance in low gravity.

His face betrayed a smile as he gazed, not noticing the increasing height of the waves until they threatened to splash over the edge. He snapped awake from his reverie, looking to the top of the staircase, seeing nothing. "Kmetra!" He shouted in frustration.

He bounded over, tripping as he climbed to the top. A figure swam awkwardly toward the center as he radioed the base for emergency lighting. Additional purplish–blue emitted at once from black stilts surrounding the telescope.

He leapt down and ran alongside the perimeter, calling her to the edge. He could see her in the reflected blue streaks of large waves, catching glimpses of the colored patchwork of her suit and arcs of light from her helmet. He tried to stay parallel to her movement.

Despite his best efforts, she seemed to be at a greater and greater distance from him. *"Kmetra!"* he yelled desperately on the radio, running around the circumference. He ultimately lost sight of her at the far side, her silhouette vanishing into eternal darkness.

Kmetra shivered violently in the shadows, her breathing ragged and heavy as she scrambled blindly uphill. The stark edge of black along the rim was still dozens of meters overhead. She felt in front of her for rocks with one hand, exhausted, plunging limbs into lunar soil.

She staggered upward, the stars disappearing from view as she neared the boundary of light. Gasping, she crossed into unforgiving sun, temporarily blinded in the vacuum of space. She shut her eyes tightly and covered her face with a free hand. The wooden doll remained with her, clutched under one arm, dusty but intact. Its glass and inner acrylic glistened in the bright starlight.

Her form was a tiny speck of color on the immense ridge above the crater. Saline crystals lined the grooves of her suit, falling from rainbowed limbs. Her helmet polarized, an organic gold color spreading over its whole surface. She opened her eyes, looking to the summit with fierce determination.

She lifted her weary body, zigzagging up the terrain, her path clearer now. She heard a warning beep and began to breath shallowly, conserving air. Her radio was muted, her heartbeat a pounding rush in her ears. She stumbled over the ridge, collapsing on the other side.

Her eyes were barely open, the border of a flat valley sideways as she lay in the dirt. Beyond the Widmanstätten patterns of an anorthosite solar field, a series of payload launchers sat at the base of foothills. She scanned the gleaming white cones in haphazard arrangement, catching sight of an older, more primitive shape. Her rapid heartbeat thudded mercilessly, overpowering the sound of her limited breathing.

She was back in the warping perspective of the night club, spectral shards whirling around her as John sat at her side on the black bank. His lips moved and he gestured in front of her as she sat, catatonic, clutching the effigy. She stared into his hands, enraptured as he mimed the shape of the vintage payload launcher, various contours in detail.

Kmetra was vertical again, taking limping leaps toward the old machine with astronaut in hand. Solar light glinted off the dome of Shackleton base behind her. Along the circumference of the crater, a small line of dust followed a vehicle as it sped around the curve.

She reached the site, weaving through the vessels to her target. She struggled with the mechanical door, turning savagely at its handles, leaning toward the hinges with forceful pulls until it swung open. She climbed halfway inside, strapping her doll securely in the only seat of the gray space, before turning to the illuminated control panel.

John scribbled on a piece of paper, her attention singularly focused among chaotic fragments of excess.

She hurriedly entered the coordinates as lights flickered in the interior. Turning over her shoulder, she saw the approaching transport and frantically set a last command before slamming the door shut. She ran for her life away from the launch pads. The vehicle braked forty meters away, its driver stepping out to intersect her path.

The blast's shockwave knocked Kmetra bodily off the ground in a plume of debris. A sharp, rocklike projectile collided with the glass of her helmet, its deafening thwack followed immediately by the hiss of rushing oxygen as she landed on her back.

A second heartbeat thudded in her ears. The gold glass marbled blue like oxidized alien copper, air bleeding from the growing fissure. Its hiss entered a spectral glide as her consciousness faded, her brown eyes fixed on her payload arcing into the heavens. A white fuzz overtook her vision as she lay a hand on her abdomen. Koji's suit came into peripheral view, a forest green glove reaching for her face as she blacked out.

polygonal static waves

                    a shining golden crackle of fabric, the pull of
rushing velocities

the dark red blur of sky against a
thick haze of dry dust

teal light rivering through the atmosphere

a blurred cerulean crescent

the backside of a waterfall

the distorted rustle of reeds in wind

Wispy white curtains billowed gently in the ventilation system, recessed aqua lighting casting a cool hue in the dark room. Kmetra rested peacefully, white bed linens rustling in the breeze.

Koji peered through a large window into the room as a medic closed the door shut behind him into the hallway.

"She's okay," The medic informed. Koji let out a huge sigh of relief through inflated cheeks, tears welling up as he stared through the glass. "She's in a coma. Her baby is fine," the medic continued as he paced the width of the hallway, swinging his arms and looking at the ceiling, "let's step over this way."

They walked together a few feet down the hall, to a round daylight window. The sun shone in black vacuum, highlighting Malapert mountain and the copper threads of Koji's ceremonial uniform. He looked down the slope, regaining control of his emotions.

"Acute hypoxia and some trauma," the medic concluded, "No brain damage though. She should wake up, but I couldn't say when. Hopefully within a few days, or weeks..." his voice trailed off, waiting a beat as Koji nodded, surveying the landscape. "Did you calculate the trajectory of the payload?"

"I sure did," Koji stroked the glass with the back of his index finger, before turning to face him. "She's a good shot... Aimed right at the source of the signals, accounting for all orbital and proper motion over time."

"How long until it reaches its destination?"

"Fifty thousand years."

***

The blue hour of twilight hung over the open top of the former greenhouse. Jupiter shone brightly and evening stars twinkled overhead. Wild ivy and overgrowth climbed the high concrete walls, bathed in yellow incandescence.

Sasha moved his hands inside an upright wooden box, starting the slow swell of music from a corner of open dirt. Lily led three residents of various ages and shades flitting through the trees in blacks and browns, impossibly weird dance movements appearing to form a single shape that spun in multiple directions.

Adjetey poked his head around the petrified door. A faint outline above him was the only remnant of the iron cage. Sasha became increasingly enraptured, moving in swing time as he played his instrument.

Lily danced in asynchronous unity, her feet slamming, then tapping Milles' dusty grave, music reverberating off the walls and into the sky.

www.ingramcontent.com/pod-product-compliance
Lightning Source LLC
Chambersburg PA
CBHW020047310726
48970CB00007B/2449